V

THE

WORLD

How to

Boost Your

Profile

hardie grant EGMONT

How to Boost Your Profile
published in 2012 by
Hardie Grant Egmont
Ground Floor, Building 1, 658 Church Street
Richmond, Victoria 3121, Australia
www.hardiegrantegmont.com.au

A CiP record for this title is available from the National Library of Australia

Text copyright © 2012 Meredith Badger
Illustration and design copyright © 2012 Hardie Grant Egmont

Design by Michelle Mackintosh
Text design and typesetting by Ektavo

Printed in Australia by Griffin Press, an Accredited ISO AS/NZS
14001:2004 Environmental Management System printer.

1 3 5 7 9 10 8 6 4 2

The paper this book is printed on is certified against the
Forest Stewardship Council® Standards. Griffin Press holds
FSC chain of custody certification SGS-COC-005088. FSC
promotes environmentally responsible, socially beneficial
and economically viable management of the world's forests.

How to Boost Your Profile

Meredith Badger

hardie grant EGMONT

One

I'm fifteen minutes early to meet Ethan for our date at the Jokey Juice bar, so I line up to get our drinks. The food court at Westland Mall is pumping with the post-school crowd and the juice queue is already winding into the sushi shop next door. Ethan and I have been going out for almost a month now, so I know exactly what to get him: apple and celery with lots of ginger.

There's a special on jumbo juices today. Directly in front of me are three primary-school girls counting up to see if they have enough for one each. They go to my old school – I recognise the cacky colours of their uniforms. One of their mums is probably shopping nearby, but I bet they're pretending that they're here alone. I used to do that too.

One of the girls has the same out-of-control curls that I had before I discovered the greatest gadget ever invented: the hair straightener. Curly-girl is the one counting the money. She looks up after a minute, eyes bright. 'We've got exactly enough!' she announces to her friends.

She's a little awkward-looking, this girl. Like she knows she's a bit nerdy but doesn't know what to do about it. Just like I used to be. I imagine going over and saying something to her. Something like, *Don't worry. When you get to high school, you can be someone different.* I picture myself producing a hair straightener from my bag and giving it to her with a smile – like a fairy god-mother – then walking away. Although I wouldn't actually walk away, because then I wouldn't be here when Ethan turns up.

Ethan. Funny how even thinking his name makes me feel quivery. I still can't believe that I actually *have* a boyfriend – I mean, out of the two hundred students in our year level, I'd say that only ten of them are going out with someone. That's only five per cent! And of that five per cent, less than half are going out with someone from our year – which means that at the school social in two weeks, Ethan and I will be one of the *only* actual couples there. That's pretty cool.

The Jokey Juice queue moves slowly forward and then finally the primary-school girls are up. The girl behind the counter is wearing an apron splattered with fruit pulp and her face is shiny with heat.

'Three jumbo apple and watermelon juices, please,' says curly-girl.

The counter girl gets busy with the juicing machine, and a few minutes later she dumps the juices down in front of the girls. I'm close enough to read today's joke printed around the bottom rim. *What time is it when an elephant sits on your fridge?* Luckily the juices here are fresher than the jokes.

Curly-girl slides across their carefully stacked pile of coins. But then there's a problem.

'You're five dollars short,' the counter girl says after counting the coins. 'The special offer ended at four.' Her thumb jabs over her shoulder. There's a clock on the wall – huge and green with a big red smiley face in the middle. 'See? It's ten past now.'

'It was before four when we got in the queue,' says curly-girl bravely.

Counter-girl shrugs. 'So?'

Curly-girl flushes and starts counting the money again. Like the coins might have somehow increased while sitting there.

I'm getting sick of this. Ethan's going to turn up soon and I don't want to be stuck in this queue when he does. I fish a five-dollar note out of my pocket and slap it onto the counter. 'Here,' I say. 'All paid for now.' The kids kind of *gape* at me but don't move, so I pick up the juices and shove them in their hands. 'Go!' I say. 'Enjoy.'

By the time I have my juices, Ethan is officially late. Only by a minute, but still, it's not like him. I check my phone, but there's no message. I could call him, I guess, but I don't want to use up my credit. Once it's gone I can't afford any more until next month. I've been trying to talk Ethan into joining the same phone company as me because then we can text each other for free. My sister Carolyn and her boyfriend Max do that, although they don't really need it because they spend every second together anyway.

I look around for somewhere to sit, but then I remember that they've just opened a new branch of Cosmetica in the mall and I may as well check it out while I'm waiting. I slip my phone into my pocket so I'll hear it when Ethan texts or calls.

The moment I walk into Cosmetica, I spot Edi, Olympia, Jess and Hazel in one corner of the shop. The *cool* girls from school. Of course they'd be here. Edi Rhineheart is one of the most stylish girls I've ever known.

'Hi, Edi!' I call. Edi says hi back but doesn't invite me to join them or anything like that. So I peer closely at the eyeliners, trying to think of a reason to go up to them.

My friends Leni and Soph hate it when I'm friendly to Edi. They've never actually *said* it, but I can tell anyway. Maybe they think I'm trying too hard or something. But I can't see what the problem is. How cool would it be if we got to join Edi's group, or even just hang with them sometimes? Or maybe Leni and Soph are worried I'll end up liking Edi and those guys better than them. I wouldn't, though.

I've just decided to go over and ask Edi if they're choosing stuff for our school social when a phone rings – not mine, unfortunately – and Edi answers.

'Yep,' she says. 'Okay, I'm coming.' Then she sighs and turns to her friends. 'I've gotta go,' she says. 'Dad's going to be out the front in five minutes.'

I call bye as Edi and the others leave, but they don't seem to hear me. It's pretty noisy in here, I guess.

There's still no sign of Ethan. I hope he's okay. He's kind of vague sometimes. Maybe he got lost. Or maybe he's been trying to text and there's something wrong with my phone. I walk around to where Edi was standing in case there's better reception in that part of the shop, and to see what she was looking at.

There's a big display promoting a new line of mascara. It's called '5000x' because it's supposed to make your eyelashes appear five thousand times longer. The girl in the poster does have amazingly long lashes, but obviously the five-thousand-times bit is an exaggeration. Because an eyelash is what – about one centimetre long? So if this mascara made them five thousand times longer, they'd be around fifty metres long. Imagine trying to blink with fifty-metre-long eyelashes! That would have to be annoying, right? The mascara does look pretty good, though. And I do need some new stuff to wear to the school social.

I put one juice down on the ground and pick up one of the mascaras. The tube is smooth and slick in my hand and I notice it has two lids – one on each end with a different-sized brush attached. That's very cool and I find myself wanting this mascara a lot. Then I check the price. It's thirty dollars. They might as well have labelled it, *Not for you, Anya Saunders.*

This is depressing. But what happens next is way worse. My phone beeps and I almost drop the mascara and the juice in my panic to get to it. Because I'm sure this will be Ethan and I've got this sudden, horrible feeling about what the message will say. Maybe something's happened to him. Something bad. Like he's been hit by a bus while hurrying to meet me. Maybe he's texting me from hospital.

But there's no need to panic. Ethan's not in the hospital. Ethan is fine. I was right about the message being something horrible, though.

Hi, Anya – sorry, but I'm not coming today. I think we should just be friends. Ethan.

I stand there with the phone in my hand, staring at it like I'm waiting for the letters to rearrange themselves into new words. Ones that don't spell out such bad news.

But the letters stay just where they are and I'm left wondering what I should do next. Maybe I should call Ethan and try to talk to him? But he might just ignore my call and that would suck. I could ring Leni or Soph, but I don't really feel like doing that either. Basically, I wish I could just disappear.

'Hey! You can't bring food or drinks in here.' One of the Cosmetica staff members – a tall girl who looks like a model – is pointing at the juices at my feet.

'Oh,' I mumble. 'Sorry.' I shove my phone away, pick up the juices again and leave the shop. Just outside the door is a bin and I dump the apple, celery and ginger juice in it. I'm glad I bought the jumbo size. It's worth the extra money for the jumbo-sized splash it makes as it hits the bottom. The cup rolls around so I see the answer to today's joke. *Time to get a new fridge.*

Jokey Juice should print up a special cup just for me. But instead of a joke of the day, they could put my photo on it.

My mum works here in the Westland Mall – not in a shop but as a receptionist in the doctor's office on the top floor. Usually I go and meet her when she finishes at five-thirty and we drive home together. But after what's happened I don't feel like hanging around in the shops anymore, so I take the elevator up to level five. Maybe Mum will be able to leave early.

Mum's standing behind the desk when I walk in. Straight away, I notice that she's got a new name badge. This one says Jillian Hoffman – her maiden name –

instead of Jillian Saunders. It makes me feel weird, looking at it. It's like my mum's suddenly a different person. It also makes me wonder. Should Carolyn and I change our names too? But Dad is still our dad, even if he's not Mum's husband anymore, and he would be pretty upset if we did. But maybe Mum will be upset if we don't.

Mum's become very skinny over the last couple of months – especially around her face – but she still looks pretty, especially when she smiles. 'Hello, honey. You're early!' she says to me. 'Weren't you meeting Ethan for a juice?'

I'm about to explain what happened when Shelley comes out of her office with a patient. 'Hi, Anya!' she says. 'When are you going to hurry up and finish medical school? I could really use another doctor around here.'

I say hi back. Shelley is the doctor Mum works for and she's really nice. She likes to be called by her first name rather than *Dr Walters*, because she says that makes her sound too old and scary. The only thing that bugs me about her is that she's got this idea I want to come and work with her as a doctor one day. Which I definitely don't. Maybe I told her once that I did when I was just a kid – but back then I thought her office was her home, and I liked the idea of living in the mall. There's no way you'd catch me dealing with sick, germy people all day. Gross!

Shelley glances around the waiting room. There's only one old woman left, sitting in the corner reading a magazine, who lets out a massive sneeze every minute or two.

'You go, Jill,' Shelley tells my mum. 'I'll close up after I've seen Mrs Carnegie.'

Even then, it takes Mum forever to shut down the computer and gather up her stuff. By the time we finally leave, I'm busting from the effort of keeping my bad news in for so long.

'Ethan and I broke up,' I say. 'He *dumped* me.'

Mum gives my shoulder a distracted little squeeze with one hand, while the other one searches for something in her bag. 'Oh sweetie,' she says. 'I'm sorry.' But I know she isn't really. The whole time I was going out with Ethan, Mum never took it seriously. I bet she thinks I'm too young to have a boyfriend. She wouldn't react like this if Carolyn broke up with Max. Everyone takes *that* relationship seriously – Carolyn makes sure of it.

Then I have an idea. A brilliant one. One that might make me feel better about the whole Ethan thing. A tiny bit, at any rate. I slip my arm through Mum's. 'You know what would cheer me up?' I say.

'An ice-cream?' suggests Mum.

I shake my head. I swear Mum still thinks I'm five sometimes. 'No. Let's go on that shopping expedition we've been planning. The shops are open for another hour.'

Mum looks confused. 'What shopping expedition?'

I can't believe she's forgotten. 'The *bra shopping* one,' I say, as patiently as I can.

I remember when Mum and Carolyn went bra shopping together. It was supposed to be this big secret but I knew exactly what was going on. They went into town together one Saturday morning and bought three bras. Then they had lunch at a fancy cafe and came home on the train together. When they walked inside, they were chatting and laughing like they'd just had the best day ever.

Carolyn was only twelve when they went, and I'm thirteen and a quarter now. I kept waiting and waiting for

Mum to say it was *our* turn to make the same trip. But she never did. I know I don't have a whole lot going on in the chest area yet, but all my friends have bras. And I know, from sneaking a look around when we're changing for sport, that there are girls at our school who are even flatter than me who wear proper bras. Basically, I'm the only girl I know who still just wears a cami top.

The thing about having a bra, which Mum doesn't seem to get, is that they make the most of what you have – so really, the flatter you are, the more reason there is to get one. That's what I think, at least. This girl Briana at our school was completely, totally flat and then she turned up one Monday morning with a proper rack. She must have got one of those padded bras – and she looked amazing.

So after months of waiting for Mum to say something, *I* had to bring the subject up with *her*. And when I did, she looked at me like I'd asked her to buy me an astronaut suit. 'But you're too young still,' she said. I then pointed out that Carolyn had been wearing bras for an entire year by my age, and Mum had kind of laughed and said, 'Okay, we'll see.'

That was weeks ago. And right now it's obvious Mum has totally forgotten the whole conversation. But this time I'm not going to let it go because I'm already picturing the look on Ethan's face when I turn up at school tomorrow with my brand-new boobs. He'll probably beg to get back with me again but I'll make him wait for ages – at least until a day or two – before I say yes.

'Please, Mum?' I say, doing my biggest, saddest, most puppy-ish eyes.

It works. Mum puts her arm around me and says, 'Let's do it.'

V

We start heading towards the lingerie section of the mall's department store. Everything's going fine until Mum's phone rings while we're on the escalator. I know straight away that it's Dad. My parents don't even bother saying hi to each other anymore. These days they just pick up the argument where they left off.

'Have you forgotten that the house is going on the

market in two weeks?' Mum says. 'The painters are coming on Thursday, Steve. The rest of your stuff better be gone by then.' She's talking in this really loud voice, and I just know that the people in front of us on the escalator are listening to every word. It's so embarrassing.

The thing is, Mum gets in such a flap whenever she starts talking about the house being sold and all the stuff that needs to be done before then, that everything else kind of fades away. I can see a simple solution: don't sell it. But whenever I suggest this, Mum says that the house has too many *associations* for her. Associations with Dad, she means. Which is funny, because it's the associations with Dad that make me *not* want it to be sold. Because that stuff only means something while it's ours.

When someone else moves into our house, they won't know that Dad laid the little blue-and-green tiles in the bathroom himself. They won't know that the wattle tree in the backyard was a present I gave Dad two years ago, and that we planted it together. And they might paint over the pencil marks on the kitchen doorframe that Dad made to measure me and Carolyn as we grew.

'Well, go over there now, then!' Mum yells suddenly as we step off the bottom of the escalator. The people in front of us look around with their eyebrows raised, but Mum doesn't even notice. Mum and Dad's 'conversations' are getting louder and louder. If they keep going like this, soon they won't need to use the phone at all – they'll just be able to yell at each other across the city.

'But you better make sure you're not damn well there when I get there tomorrow afternoon.' Except Mum doesn't say *damn well*. She says a way worse word.

'Well, really!' the woman in front of us mutters.

To block it out, I start thinking about what kind of bra I'm going to buy. It's something I've thought about a lot lately. I've been looking online and measuring myself weekly with a tape measure to make sure I know exactly what size to get. The other 'research' I've been doing is trying on Carolyn's bras when she's not around. She's got heaps of nice ones but my favourite is a white satin one with silver sparkles. It was my dream bra for a long time. If I do it up on the smallest hooks and pull my shoulders way back, I can make it stay up.

But then I found an ad in a magazine for a bra that was even better than Carolyn's sparkly one. The ad is divided into two. On one side there's a girl walking through school with a smile on her face, her hair billowing back and her tight top showing off her amazing figure. There's a group of students in the background staring at her admiringly (the boys) and jealously (the girls). On the other half of the ad, you see a close-up of the bra itself. It's purple satin with tiny diamantés scattered across it like little stars. The cups are padded and there are arrows on the ad showing how this bra pushes your boobs up and makes the most of what you've got. *Boost your profile with the Charm Bra* says the ad at the bottom.

Mum is still on the phone to Dad when we get to the lingerie department, so I give her my pleading look again and she tells Dad that he'll have to call back later.

'Right,' she says, putting the phone away. 'Where do we start?'

At the moment we are surrounded by the most massive beige bras I've ever seen. I can't imagine anyone having breasts large enough to fill them. There's one near me that's so huge my whole head would fit in one of the cups.

Mum looks around. 'We need to find an attendant,' she says. I try to explain that we don't need help because I already know what style and size I want. We just need to find the bras that aren't big enough to live in and I'll be fine. But as usual Mum isn't listening. She spots a woman with a name badge and starts waving. 'Excuse me!' she calls loudly. 'Can you come and measure my daughter for her first bra?'

I want to die. 'Mum!' I hiss. 'I don't *need* to be measured. I know all that already.' But it's too late by then – the woman is already coming over. She's got grandmother-like short grey hair and there's a tape measure draped around her neck. Looking at her, I suddenly realise who those massive bras are made for. It seems unfair – like this lady has been greedy and taken more than her share and left me with hardly anything.

She smiles at me. 'So, it's your first bra, dear? How exciting!' She's speaking just as loudly as Mum was.

I'm too mortified to do anything but nod. This is not how I imagined the shopping trip going.

'Of course,' says Mum, 'she doesn't really need one yet,

but we thought we'd get one anyway.'

'Oh, we'll find one that fits,' says the assistant. 'I'll just check what size we need.'

And before I really understand what's happening, she's whipped her tape measure off her neck and wrapped it around my chest, right across my nipples, and then again beneath my breasts. She does it so fast it's like a magic trick.

'We'll start with an 8A, shall we?' she announces, so that Mum (and probably the entire shop) can hear.

I shake my head. 'No, I'll need a B cup,' I say. 'At least.' Carolyn wears a B and, seriously, it's not *that* much too big for me. But the sales assistant and Mum both laugh like it's the funniest thing they've ever heard.

'We'll see how we go, shall we, pet,' says the assistant.

She leads us over to the teen section where I'm relieved to see that the bras look much more normal-sized. And I suddenly spot it. The *Charm Bra*. It's even more perfect in real life than it looked in the ad.

Mum has walked on ahead with the assistant, so I call her and hold up the dream bra. 'Mum!' I say. 'This is the one I want.'

Mum's smile goes a little wonky then, like it's trying to turn downwards but she's forcing it to stay up. 'That one?' she says. 'Really?'

'Yes, really,' I say. 'Isn't it awesome?'

Mum's smile fades completely. 'Honey, I don't think it'll fit you.'

But I know she's wrong. 'I'm going to try it on,' I say, looking around for the change rooms. I can't wait to see what my profile looks like.

'Can I have a look at it?' says Mum, walking back towards me. She examines it like it's a particularly germy patient in the waiting room – one she doesn't want to come too close. 'It's very … shiny,' she says. When she spots the price tag, she sucks in her breath. 'Outrageous!' she murmurs, putting the bra back on the nearest rack. 'So much money for something so tacky.'

I take it back off the rack. 'Carolyn has bras like this,' I point out.

'Carolyn has a job,' Mum shoots right back at me. 'She buys her own bras.' Mum sighs. 'There's no way I can afford this, Anya. I'm sorry.' It's that same *sorry* she used when I told her about breaking up with Ethan. The one that means she isn't really sorry at all.

'You wouldn't buy it even if you could afford it, would you?' I say. I know this sounds sulky – which Mum hates – but I can't help it. I *feel* sulky.

'No,' agrees Mum. 'I wouldn't. It's not appropriate for someone your age to be wearing a padded bra. Thirteen-year-olds should look like thirteen-year-olds, not twenty-year-olds.'

This is so frustrating! I want to point out that heaps of girls my age wear bras like this, but just then the sales assistant comes over.

'How about these?' she says, holding up two of the plainest bras I've ever seen in my life. One is pale grey and the other one is white. There's not even the smallest amount of padding on either of them. No decoration. I feel myself dying of boredom just looking at them. There's no way these bras will *boost my profile* at all.

But Mum nods and says, 'Perfect.'

The attendant leads me over to the fitting rooms and then guards the door so I can't escape.

It's while I'm in there that I see something. Something a little scary. I noticed a while ago that my left breast is smaller than my right one. Like, noticeably smaller. But in the bright lights of the change room, I see something else that's weird about leftie – there's this blue vein running up the side of it, really close to the skin. I check the right one, but I can't see a vein on that side. That seems wrong and I start thinking, *Maybe the vein is somehow connected to the smallness? Maybe leftie will never grow any bigger? Maybe I've got some kind of disease?*

I look at it for a minute, wondering if I should yell out to Mum. But then the shop attendant would probably come in too and I don't want that. In fact, I don't really want to think about the vein at all. I quickly get back into my clothes and get out of there.

'You were supposed to call us when you had them on!' says the attendant.

'Sorry,' I mutter.

'So are we getting them or not?' says my mum. 'The shop is closing soon.'

'I guess so,' I say, handing them over. I figure ugly bras

are better than no bras. *Slightly* better – in the way that having your foot amputated is slightly better than having your whole leg removed.

The attendant chats away to Mum while she does the sale – like this has all been a huge success.

Then she puts the bras in a bag and hands it over to me. 'Cheer up, pet!' she says. 'It's not that bad.'

Cheer up? I want to yell. *Would you be cheerful if you'd just been dumped via text message? Would you be cheerful if you found a weird blue vein on your breast that probably means you've got some horrible disease?* But I don't say it because I don't want to freak Mum out. Anyway, the attendant isn't even looking at me. She's staring at the bag, frowning.

'I did take the security tag off, didn't I?' she says. 'If you leave the shop with them still on, they make a terrible racket.'

Mum checks the bag. The tags are off, which is good. This day has been terrible enough without me setting off a bunch of alarms.

As we leave, I ask Mum where she's taking me for dinner.

'What do you mean, honey?' she says.

I remind her that when she and Carolyn went bra shopping, they went out for lunch afterwards. Mum sighs and pushes her hair up from her forehead. Her fringe hovers for a moment before crashing like a wave back over her face.

'Oh sweetie,' she says. 'Not tonight, okay? I'm so tired. We'll go out another time, I promise.'

I don't say anything. Not, *You're always tired*, or, *That's so not fair*, even though both those things are true. Because I know there's nothing I can say that will change her mind.

We end up buying Thai and taking it back to the flat to eat in front of the television, like we do every night. Carolyn has just finished washing her hair when we get home and she's sitting on the couch, combing it. She has completely straight hair and only has to blow-dry it, like Mum, while I inherited Dad's crazy waves.

'Where've you guys been?' she asks. Mum makes me show her the bras we bought.

'Oh, aren't they *cute!*' Carolyn says in this completely fake way of hers which only I ever notice.

'They're nice, aren't they?' says Mum.

Then Max calls and Carolyn takes her food into her room so she can talk to him while she eats. Because, you know, she hasn't seen him for a couple of hours.

I don't eat much dinner. Maybe it's because the smell of the ginger in Mum's laksa reminds me of Ethan's favourite juice. Maybe it's because I still haven't got used to how big our sofa looks in this little room – like an ocean liner stuck in a duck pond. Or maybe it's because I keep thinking about the vein, wondering what it means.

Mum falls asleep on the couch as usual, so I take the containers out to the kitchen and then go to my room.

I lie on my bed for a while, looking through my phone at all the messages Ethan and I have exchanged over the last twenty-eight days. I look at that last one he sent me over and over, trying to think of a reply. Usually my problem is trying to *stop* texting. But right now, when it really matters, I can't think of a thing to say.

Three

I wake up the next morning to the sound of the shower pounding away. It's Carolyn, using up all the hot water again. Mum is clanging about in the kitchen. I know what that clanging means. Because we still haven't unpacked everything yet, Mum often has trouble finding stuff. And when Mum can't find stuff, she starts blaming Dad.

I sit up and check my phone, in case Ethan has texted me during the night to say, *Sorry, I made a big mistake and I hope you'll take me back*. He hasn't, though. But suddenly I feel like I'm ready to tell my friends about it.

Ethan dumped me, I text Leni and Soph. *By text msg!!!
Can u believe it???*

My friends are quick to reply – even Soph, who is usually hopelessly slow.

Soph writes: *What a loser. You're better off without him.*

Leni writes: *Oh no! :(Wish I could hug u.*

The messages make me feel a little better. My friends are so great.

The bathroom door finally clicks open. I hop out of bed and wrap myself in my bathrobe. It's a big white fluffy one that I got for my thirteenth birthday. Whenever I wear it I feel like I'm a guest in some cool hotel.

'Hi, Mum,' I call as I pad past the kitchen on the way to the shower.

'I *still* can't find the iron!' Mum replies, shaking her head in disbelief. 'Your father must have taken it. Ridiculous! He's never ironed anything in his life!'

'Maybe he thought it was a sandwich toaster?' I suggest. It makes Mum laugh, but I instantly feel a bit guilty. It's like I've taken sides against Dad or something by saying it.

After my (lukewarm) shower I go back to my room

and check for the vein on leftie. It's still there and I get this funny feeling in my stomach, looking at it. Like I can't deal with thinking about it right now. I quickly grab a new bra – the white one – and put it on. If I can't see the vein, maybe I won't worry about it. Whenever I try on one of Carolyn's bras I have to swivel it around so that the doing-uppy bits are in the front. But today I'm determined to do my new bra up at the back, no swivelling. Carolyn's bras usually have two hooks, but mine only has one. I do it up without looking, no problem at all.

That's the only good thing about this dumb bra, though. In every other way it's a complete dud. I pull on my school uniform and then look in my mirror, standing side-ways. My profile hasn't been boosted *at all*. If anything, my chest looks even flatter than before. If Mum had bought me the Charm Bra, I just know Ethan would have fallen over himself to get back with me. This bra might make Ethan fall over too – but from laughing. That's if he notices at all.

My jumper is underneath my blazer on my chair, and as I grab it something falls from the blazer pocket and lands near my foot. I stare down and for a few moments it's like my brain can't actually register what it's seeing. Because the thing that's fallen from my pocket makes no sense. It's the 5000+ mascara from Cosmetica.

My first thought is that maybe Mum bought it for me to say she was sorry I had such a bad day yesterday. But this is very unlikely. Mum hates me wearing make-up and she'd never spend thirty dollars on mascara, even for herself. And then I realise what's happened. I must have accidentally put the mascara into my pocket when I was in Cosmetica yesterday.

I pick up the mascara, feeling weird. I didn't take it on purpose, but I still left the shop without paying for it. Does this make me a thief? My heart loops. What if someone saw me? What if they're waiting for me to come back to the shop so they can arrest me? But this is dumb. If anyone had seen me take it they would've said something straight away. And once I've calmed down a bit, I realise there's an easy way to fix this situation. I zip the tube into the pocket of my uniform. The next time I'm at the mall I'll take it back to Cosmetica and just explain what happened.

When I get to the kitchen Carolyn is in there, eating

toast and fiddling with her phone. I hear banging noises from Mum's room and I know she's hurrying to get to work. Some days she gives us a lift to school, but on days like today when she starts early we walk or catch the bus.

'Hi,' I say to Carolyn, reaching for the cereal.

She ignores me, as usual. Mum told me once that Carolyn gets a bit moody just before her period, but that means she must be getting it pretty much constantly. Anyway, I don't get like that when I get mine. Carolyn has changed. Sometimes I can't believe she's the same person I used to look up to so much that I would to cry when she went away on school camp.

'*Hi*,' I say again. Loudly.

Carolyn puts down her phone and flashes me a phony smile. 'Hiya, mathlete!' she says. My sister knows exactly what to say to make me mad. And nothing makes me madder than being called *mathlete*. That word makes me feel like I'm a frizzy-haired freak again, back in a daggy, cacky-brown uniform.

'I'm not a mathlete anymore!' I yell at her. 'That was three years ago!'

'Once a mathlete, always a mathlete,' says Carolyn in this sing-song voice that I hate.

'That's not true, spazmo!'

Mum comes clumping in then, a hairbrush in one hand and bobby pins in the other. 'Anya!' she says. 'Don't use that awful word. And don't shout.' Because this is always how it works in our house at the moment. Carolyn winds me up and then *I* get told off when I snap.

'It's Carolyn's fault,' I say.

Carolyn shrugs, like she's completely baffled. 'I was just asking Anya about that maths competition she helped organise back in primary school,' she says. 'Remember how proud everyone was of her for coming up with such a clever idea?'

Mum starts shoving bobby pins in her hair, using the window behind the kitchen sink as a mirror. 'We were all very proud,' she agrees. 'Anya won lots of medals.'

'You should organise another maths competition for this year too,' Carolyn says to me. 'I bet Mr Cartright would be totally into it. And then you'd get to show everyone in high school how brainy and good at maths you are, just like you did at primary school.'

I'm ready to *destroy* my sister now, but I know that it will only get me into more trouble with Mum. So I take a deep breath. 'How many times do I have to tell you that I'm not good at maths anymore?' I say, through gritted teeth. 'High-school maths is much harder than primary-school maths. I'm only just passing.'

Mum gives me a concerned look. 'Are you struggling, honey?' she says. 'Maybe I should make an appointment to see your maths teacher.'

'It's okay, Mum,' I say hastily, although I know there's no real danger of this happening. Mum doesn't have time to get a haircut, let alone set up meetings at school. 'Just don't expect me to get A's in maths like I used to.' I dump cereal into my bowl and splash some milk on top. 'Especially at the moment – because of breaking up with Ethan.'

I am stupid enough to think that when Carolyn hears this, she might actually feel a little sorry for me. I should know better.

'Aw, the Wonder Dork dumped you at last, then?' says Carolyn, picking up her phone.

'Ethan is *not* a dork!' I say. It's true that he used to be a *little* dorky before we started going out, but I upgraded him. I showed him a cooler way of doing his hair and told him not to keep pens clipped to his blazer pocket anymore.

'You'll get over it pretty quick,' says Carolyn. 'It's not like it was a *real* relationship.'

This is so annoying. Just because I didn't go out with Ethan for as long as Carolyn has been seeing Max doesn't mean it wasn't real. It felt real to me. And knowing that I now have to go to the school social *alone* feels real, too.

To make things worse, Mum just sighs and says, 'Just for once it would be nice to have breakfast without some ridiculous teenage drama taking place.' Then she gives us both a quick peck on the cheek and says, 'Don't forget you're staying at your father's place tonight. He's going to pick you up after school.'

'I'm working after school,' Carolyn says. She has a job as a sales assistant at a shop called Tude. The clothes are pretty cool – and really expensive. 'I'll go to Dad's place afterwards.'

Mum frowns at Carolyn. 'You're not supposed to work

during the week. You'll get behind at school.'

'Mum, it's important that I'm there tonight,' Carolyn pleads. 'The buyer is coming in with some of the spring samples and I really want to meet her.'

'What is a buyer?' says Mum. I'm glad she's asked, because I have no idea either.

'She's the person who goes around the world sourcing things for us to sell in the shop,' says Carolyn. It's the most excited I've seen her in ages. 'It's the best job. I really want to meet her and ask her about how you get to be one.'

Mum pulls a face. 'That's not the sort of career I'd like you to have,' she says.

Carolyn pulls a face too. 'Well, it's the sort of career *I'd* like to have!' she says. 'And it's *my* life.'

Mum opens her mouth and I know that if she says one more word, there's going to be a huge fight. I don't think I can handle any more fighting right now.

'Mum,' I say, pointing to the kitchen clock, which is propped up against the spice rack because no-one's got around to fixing it to the wall. 'If you don't go now you're going to be late.'

Mum glances at the time and sees that I'm right. She picks up her coffee-to-go cup and heads for the door. 'We'll talk about this later, Carolyn,' she calls out.

Once she's gone I look at Carolyn, waiting for her to thank me for stopping the fight when I did. But my darling sister just screws up her face and says, 'What are you looking at?'

Usually when she says this, I say, *I haven't worked it out yet.* But right now I can't be bothered saying anything to her. I feel heavy, like I've just eaten twenty bowls of cereal instead of just a couple of mouthfuls. Silently, I get up and go to my room where I plug in my hair straightener.

While it warms up, I start my make-up. A thick layer of foundation goes on first to cover up the red blotches on my cheeks. Then there's concealer for the circles under my eyes. Rouge, so I don't look so washed out. Eye shadow, with separate colours for the brow, the corner and the bit just above my eye. Putting on make-up always makes me feel good. It doesn't even matter that by recess, some teacher will make me wash it off. It's putting it on that counts. I know Leni and Soph think it's a waste of time, but they don't get it. Putting on make-up is like covering up the bad stuff. It's the same with my hair. My dumb curls are the one thing I know I can smooth out.

I've still got a tube of old, cheap mascara in my make-up bag, but when it's time to apply it I find myself pulling out the 5000x from my pocket. I hold it in my hand. Does it really matter if I keep it? Cosmetica has hundreds of branches. And each shop must have at least fifty tubes of this mascara. It's not like they'll miss one little tube. I twist it and crack the plastic seal.

The 5000x mascara is incredible. *Way* better than my old one. It's thick and lush and, although it doesn't make my eyelashes look 50 metres long (which I'm glad about, really), they definitely look very cool.

When I'm finished, I open up my cupboard and look at myself in the full-length mirror stuck to the door. Maybe my boobs don't look any bigger, but I feel like my profile has been boosted a little.

Four

I spot Leni and Soph before they see me. Leni, who is tall and totally gorgeous (although she has no idea that she is), has her sports bag slung over her shoulder so I guess she's had an early training session with the aths team this morning. Soph is munching on something that looks way too healthy and homemade for my liking, and she's talking very intently to Leni. Probably about her latest plans to save the world.

Sometimes I think it's weird that the three of us are friends. It's not like we have a whole lot in common. For instance, I can't drag either of them into Cosmetica, even if I try bribing them with the promise of a Jokey Juice afterwards. And the things they're into don't exactly light my fire either. I went on a protest march with Soph and her mum once and it was the most boring thing I've ever done – although I made sure she didn't realise that.

I figure friendship is something you just shouldn't examine too much. It's like gravity – you just accept that it works, even if you don't understand exactly how. Because if you start questioning it, maybe you'll end up floating away into space. I'm just happy I've got Leni and Soph.

I sneak towards them until I'm really close. Then I yell, 'Hi, guys!' and pull them towards me so that our heads almost collide. Leni yelps in surprise and Soph drops what she's eating.

'Anya!' says Soph crossly. 'That was my breakfast!' The thing on the ground looks kind of like a muesli bar, but a mutant one. There are all these green, bug-like seeds sticking out of it and it's a safe bet there's no chocolate.

'Um – I think I've done you a favour, Soph,' I say, crossing my eyes at her. Soph never stays mad at me for very long – especially if I can make her laugh. 'But hey,'

I add, because I feel bad about making her lose her breakfast even if it does look gross, 'I've got a *real* muesli bar in my bag. You can have it if you want.' I fish it out from where it's lurking, way down the bottom. There's a splodge of something blue and sticky on it – probably from the leaky pen in the bottom of my bag that I keep forgetting to remove. 'Mmm, this one is ink-flavoured!' I say, offering it to her. 'Nommy-nommy!'

Soph backs away, laughing like I knew she would. 'No, thanks,' she says. 'I was full anyway.'

'So you and Ethan really broke up?' says Leni. 'I can't believe it.'

I nod and then sit down on the grass. Leni and Soph sit beside me and I show them Ethan's message. They both agree that it was really low of him to send it instead of talking to me about it in person.

'What did you write back?' asks Soph.

They can't believe it when I tell them I haven't written anything yet. 'I just haven't worked out what to say,' I explain. 'I guess I'm still in shock.' I lie back on the ground, even though there's a risk that the dampness from the grass will make my hair revert to a giant frizzball. 'And the worst bit is that now I can't go to the social anymore,' I sigh.

'Why not?' asks Soph in surprise.

It seems pretty obvious to me why not, but I explain anyway. How I've been picturing the social for so long in my head. Me turning up in some amazing dress, my arm tucked through Ethan's, everyone looking at us enviously. 'It won't be any fun going on my own,' I say.

'You won't be going on your own,' says Leni, giving me a gentle push. 'You'll be going with *us*. Your friends. It'll be way more fun. At least Soph and I know how to *dance*.'

That makes me laugh, because Ethan is definitely not the most co-ordinated person. 'Okay,' I say, sitting up and brushing the grass off my back. 'I'll come.'

Leni's right. It will be fun going with them. Plus it'll give me a chance to look *amazing* in front of Ethan, so he realises what a big mistake he's made.

'I just can't work out *why* Ethan did it,' I say. 'It was just so *sudden*. What happened?'

The tiniest flicker of a look passes between Leni and Soph – one I'm not meant to see.

'You guys know something, don't you?' I say, pouncing immediately. 'Come on. Tell me.'

Leni suddenly looks really uncomfortable and I know it'll be hard to get any info out of her – especially if she thinks it's going to hurt my feelings. So I turn to Soph, who is big on telling things as they are even if it's painful. 'Spill it, Soph,' I say.

'We saw Ethan just before you turned up this morning,' says Soph. 'He was walking with Hannah Darcy.'

I can't believe it. '*Massive* Hannah?' I say. 'You're kidding me, right? Were they holding hands?'

'Shh!' say Soph, looking around.

'No, they weren't doing anything like that,' says Leni soothingly. 'They were just walking together, laughing about something.'

Walking and laughing with someone doesn't necessarily mean anything, but then sometimes it does. The thing is, Ethan never really laughed much with me at all. Half the time I wasn't even sure he was listening, which is why I had to send him so many text messages.

I take a breath. Try to calm down. 'Are you *sure* it was

Hannah?' I say. It's pretty awful to be text-dumped by your boyfriend. But when it looks like you might have been replaced by someone like her – well, that's just too much. It's not just that she's really huge, it's also that she's one of the nerdiest people in our entire year. She always sits up the front in class and asks way too many questions. The only person I can think of who is nerdier than Hannah is … well, Ethan, I guess, but back before I changed him. I can't believe that he would give me up to go out with her. It's so humiliating.

'We're sure,' says Soph quietly. Leni pulls a sympathetic face and nods.

I take out my phone.

'What are you doing?' asks Soph.

'I'm texting Ethan, of course,' I say. 'I have to find out if he's going out with Hannah now.'

'No, don't,' says Soph quickly, grabbing my phone.

Leni agrees with her. 'Wait till you've calmed down a bit at least,' she says. 'Otherwise you might say something you regret.' Right now I can't imagine regretting anything I might say to Ethan.

The bell rings and Soph gets up. 'We'd better go,' she says. 'It's maths first and you know how Mr Cartright loves giving out detention if you're late.' Actually, Mr Cartright loves giving out detention even if you blink at the wrong time during his class.

Soph makes me promise I'll just ignore Ethan for the moment before she gives back my phone. 'Don't let him see that you're upset about this,' she says.

I shove my phone in my bag, then sling my schoolbag onto my shoulder. 'Oh, don't worry – I'll ignore him, all right,' I say. 'I'll ignore him like no-one has ever ignored him before.'

Ethan is sitting back where he used to sit before we started going out – right at the front of class. Hannah is beside him. So Leni and Soph were right. I instantly start ignoring him. I hope he notices.

We make it to our seats just before Mr Cartright strides in. He's been at the school for about a hundred years and he has a beard that stretches from ear to ear but no moustache, which looks totally wrong to me. He also has these really thick woolly eyebrows that meet in the middle. It's like he's tried to grow a moustache, but just too high up on his face. Mr Cartright doesn't like me and the feeling is completely mutual. He's so different to Miss Smith, who was the teacher who made me love maths back at primary school. Maths was fun back then – because Miss Smith always came up with interesting activities for us to do. Mr Cartright's classes are always exactly the same. He stands up the front and writes down an example of something on the whiteboard, then sets us problems to do. It's so predictable and boring.

Mr Cartright has favourites, too. He gives them extra work and gets them to compete in maths competitions and stuff. Ethan's one of his favourites and Hannah is another. I've worked very hard *not* to be one. I guess I was kind of Miss Smith's favourite and I got teased about it heaps. After that I realised it's better to be ordinary, which is basically what I've aimed for ever since I started high school.

When Mr Cartright starts droning on, I begin

calculating how long it'll take me to save up my pocket money to buy a Charm Bra. I have to take into account my essentials, like credit for my phone and Jokey Juices, but I also think about ways I can save money, like asking for the bus fare from Mum and then walking to school instead. I've just come up with the answer – about three months – when Soph hisses, 'Anya!'

I sit up with a start, realising that Mr Cartright has asked me a question and everyone is looking at me, waiting for me to answer. Everyone except Ethan, who is keeping his eyes straight ahead.

'I'm sorry, Mr Cartright,' I say. 'Could you repeat that?'

Mr Cartright's eyebrows scrunch down like grey storm clouds and he raps the whiteboard with a marker pen. 'What does x equal in this equation?' he says. 'You'll need to apply the formula we learnt yesterday.'

I look at the board and work out the answer, pretty much straight away. I think about pretending I have no idea, but I'm feeling a little flustered so I just blurt it out instead. 'X equals 16.'

Mr Cartright opens his mouth, like he's about to tell

me off for getting it wrong like I usually do (on purpose), and then realises I've said the right answer. The look on his face is pretty funny, and I guess I must smirk or something because suddenly he glares at me. 'What is that gunk on your face, young lady?'

Oops. I thought I was sitting too far away for him to notice my make-up. His eyesight must be better than I realised.

'Go and wash it off. Now.'

I make my chair scrape loudly across the floor as I stand up and start to walk towards the door.

Mr Cartright has already turned his attention back to the class. 'Anyone else have an idea about this next equation?'

Hannah's hand shoots into the air, which is typical, but I'm surprised (and frankly, disappointed) when Leni also puts her hand up. I need to talk to her about this. She's going to end up a favourite if she's not careful.

I deliberately walk right in front of where Ethan is sitting and, although he's not looking at me, I give him an extremely disdainful look before I walk out the door.

Even if he didn't see it, I'm sure he must have felt it burning the back of his neck.

V

Edi Rhineheart is in the girls' bathrooms when I get there and for once she's not surrounded by her entourage. She's drying her hands and on her wrist is a pretty silver bracelet, gleaming in the light. It's made from several threads all twisted and knotted together. It's so beautiful that I can't stop staring at it. Maybe I'd feel – and look – just a tiny bit more like Edi if I had a bracelet like that, something that sparkled and shone.

'I love your bracelet,' I say.

'Thanks.' Edi isn't looking at me when she replies but then, she never really is. Sometimes I suspect that she doesn't even know my name. 'Do you know that shop Cargo?'

I nod. 'It's that little cool one near the cinema, right?' I don't bother adding *expensive*.

'Yep,' says Edi. 'It's from there.'

This is the longest conversation I've ever had with

Edi. And it's going pretty well so far. I lean against the nearest sink and sigh. 'Mr Cartright is making me wash off my make-up,' I say. Edi makes a sympathetic noise and straightens her skirt. I can tell she's about to leave. 'I'm kind of spewing,' I add quickly, 'because the mascara is 5000x and I hate to waste it.'

Edi turns around then and looks at me. *Really* looks at me. 'You've got some 5000x?'

I shrug, like it's no big deal. 'Sure,' I say, 'It's the best one.'

Edi stares at my eyelashes for so long that I start to feel a little self-conscious. 'I mean, obviously it doesn't really make them look five thousand times longer,' I say, babbling a little, 'because that would be crazy. But still.'

'It looks great,' says Edi. 'I'll have to get some!'

Without thinking twice about it, I unzip the pocket of my uniform and pull out the 5000x and hand it to Edi. 'Here. You have it.'

She stares at me in astonishment. 'No way. Really?'

'Sure,' I say. 'My mum and my sister both work at the mall. I get a huge discount on anything I buy.' Okay, so it's a lie – but it's worth it when Edi smiles at me.

'Well, if you're sure,' she says, taking the 5000x. 'Thanks!'

As she walks out, she stops and says, 'It's Anya, right?'

'Right.'

'Well, see you round, Anya.'

I say *See you round* back. Then I get to work, scrubbing off the make-up, but I don't mind because I'm busy thinking. I'm thinking about how *easy* it was to take the 5000x. How I'd done it without even realising. Would it be just as easy if I actually *meant* to steal something? It's a pretty interesting question.

Five

For the rest of the day, I sneak looks at Ethan during class, but every time, he seems to be totally focused on his work. Not once do I catch him taking a peek at me. And during the breaks he disappears completely. It's so frustrating! How am I supposed to ignore someone who is avoiding me? Leni and Soph keep saying it's better this way, but I don't see why. The more time goes by, the more confused I feel about what went wrong between us. I just can't work out why he'd choose Hannah over me.

I admit that the way we got together was a bit unusual.

I had this idea for a kissing competition, which I basically came up with as a way of helping my friends. They are both such awesome people but they're completely hopeless when it comes to guys. Leni just turns every boy she knows into a friend, even when it's obvious (to me at least) that they have a *thing* for her. And Soph is too focused on all her campaigns and issues to bother with guys. I mean, that's not right, is it? I love imagining us all going out together with our boyfriends – to the movies or to the Royal Show or whatever. But I realised that this was never going to happen unless I helped them out.

So to give them a push-start, I decided that we all had two weeks to kiss someone – and this is how I ended up kissing Ethan. His mum is friends with my mum so I've known him since primary school. I always thought he was a total dork, but that changed after we kissed. I guess I started seeing beyond the geeky exterior and realised that with a bit of work, Ethan had the potential to be really hot. And the thing is, the more time I spent with him the more I *liked* him. He's funny, you know, in a quiet kind of way. And he sometimes came out with stuff that really surprised me. Like one day last week, after I'd had a massive fight with Carolyn, he said to me, 'You know she deliberately stirs you up because she's jealous of you.'

Interesting, huh? I mean, obviously it isn't true. Why would Carolyn be jealous of me, for god's sake? But I was still pretty blown away. I've known him for ages but I never realised he thought about things like that. So you can see why I was upset about being dumped – especially with no explanation.

Anyway, the whole day goes past and it's like I no longer exist for Ethan. It's awful, and by the time I walk out of the gates to meet Dad after school, I'm feeling kind of low.

Dad's already there, waiting in his van – I can see him through the window looking at something on his phone. The van has *Mick's Insulation* written across the side in big red letters, even though my dad isn't called Mick. In fact, there is no Mick at the insulation company he works for at all. Dad says it's just a name the owner came up with because Mick sounds like the sort of person you'd trust to go in your roof. The owner's name is Cyril and he definitely doesn't look like a guy you want anywhere near your roof. Whenever I've met him at the main office he's been running around, looking worried. Dad calls him Cyril the Squirrel, but not to his face.

When Dad sees me, he leans over and opens the front passenger door. This is usually Carolyn's seat and if she catches me in it, I'm dead meat. Dad sees me hesitate and smiles. 'Don't worry, kiddo,' he says. 'She's working this afternoon.'

I'm surprised to hear this after what Mum said at breakfast. But I can already guess what's happened. Carolyn rang Dad to ask if it was okay just this once, and Dad gave in. Not that I mind. An afternoon without Carolyn sounds fine to me.

I slip into the seat beside Dad, glad that for once I don't have to sit on the fold-down seat in the back with all of Dad's tools sliding around at my feet.

'How about we catch a film?' says Dad. 'I just checked the listings – there's a new *Princess Paula* movie at four-thirty. You like those *Princess Paula* movies, don't you?'

Okay, so maybe I used to like *Princess Paula* movies – when I was seven. But I can't point this out to Dad because he seems genuinely excited about going. 'Well, that sounds great,' I say, 'but I've got a whole heap of homework …'

Dad swats my excuse away with one hand. 'Don't worry about that,' he says. 'How often do we get a chance to go to a film together, just you and me?' I give up thinking of excuses after that.

We round a corner and all Dad's work stuff slides back to the other side of the van. 'Hey, kiddo, here's a problem for you,' says Dad. 'I have a big job on tomorrow – the roof is fifteen metres by eighteen metres. How many square metres of insulation do you reckon I'll need?'

I groan. 'Dad! I've already had a maths lesson today. I don't need another one.'

'You used to think that working stuff out for me was fun,' Dad says, and I can tell from his voice he's a little offended. It's true that I used to like helping Dad with his calculations. He'd pretend that he wasn't working for Cyril the Squirrel anymore and had started his own business with me as his assistant. I loved spending the day driving around with my dad, helping him work stuff out. But that was when I was just a kid.

'Sorry, Dad – I guess I just don't find it interesting anymore,' I say.

At the cinema, Dad goes down into the underground parking. Mum never does that. She always parks miles away where she doesn't have to pay for a ticket and makes us walk. And she always brings snacks from home too, instead of letting us buy things at the cinema snack bar.

When we get to the cinema, I'm surprised by how many people are queuing up for tickets. They don't look like the typical *Princess Paula* crowd either. But then I look at the board and realise that there's another movie screening at the same time. It's called *Creature from the Black Lagoon* and suddenly I remember that the one time Ethan and I went to see a movie together, he got all excited when he saw the poster for it.

'That's a classic sci-fi film!' he said. 'I can't believe they're showing it here. I'd love to see it.' It didn't look like my sort of thing at all, so I told Ethan there was no way I was going. He looked kind of disappointed, but didn't mention it again. The funny thing is that just as I'm remembering this, I spot a familiar sandy-coloured head of hair in the ticket queue and sure enough, it's Ethan. Standing beside him is Hannah Darcy.

My heart slides down my body and down into my toes. It's obvious that something is going on between them. It's not that they're kissing or even touching or anything. But they just look comfortable together. Hannah is talking and Ethan is smiling and really paying attention to everything she says. I don't remember Ethan ever looking at *me* the way he's looking at Hannah.

'Dad, I have to go to the toilet,' I mutter. Because I need to get away from this. Need a moment alone to get a grip. What I really want is to run from the cinema as fast as I can but I can't, of course.

'Are you okay, kiddo?' Dad asks. 'You look a bit pale.'

'Yeah, I'm fine,' I mutter and then rush to the loo before Ethan sees me. Looks like *I'm* doing the avoiding now.

The toilets are like a dimly lit time machine, piping in hit songs from the eighties. I catch a glimpse of my reflection in one of the mirrors. My hair has started to frizz and my make-up-free face looks completely washed-out.

No wonder Ethan dumped me. I'd dump me too.

I lock myself in one of the cubicles and sit on the toilet with the lid down. There's a sign stuck to the wall with a picture of a shadowy hand reaching under a door and grabbing a bag. *Thieves use the toilet too!* it says. The walls of the cubicle are covered with grafitti. The usual stuff – *HR + NF* and *I ♡ Archie de Souza*. And there, just above the toilet roll, is *Anya 4 Ethan*. I'd forgotten I'd done that. I stare at it for a long time, remembering how good I'd felt writing it, putting my name up there with all those other names. Then I take my keys from my pocket and use them to scratch the letters off again. All that's left when I'm done is a big horrible mess.

Someone raps loudly on the door. 'Is anyone even in there? There's a big queue of people waiting out here.'

'Hang on!' I yell back. 'I'm almost done.' I jump up hurriedly and flush the toilet, so no-one will guess I was just sitting here scratching paint. I flick my hair behind my shoulders as I undo the lock. There's a woman waiting on the other side, arms folded impatiently. 'Sorry,' I say apologetically. 'I don't feel very well.' Maybe that will make her feel guilty for hassling me.

When I get back to the cinema foyer I see that Dad is still halfway along the queue, checking his phone. I know I should go and stand with him, but Ethan could be anywhere and I'm totally not in the mood for running into him and Hannah together. Not yet.

Then I realise I'm standing right in front of Cargo – the shop where Edi's pretty bracelet came from.

I find the bracelet lying on top of a display case at the back of the shop. Someone must have been trying it on and the shop assistant forgot to lock it back in the case. I look over to the desk, wondering if it's okay if I try it on. The shop assistant is busy with a customer. There are a heap of brightly coloured scarves lying in a heap on the counter like a melted rainbow. The customer has a bright pink one wrapped around her neck, and she's looking at herself this way and that in the mirror.

'These scarves are so beautiful,' the shop assistant is saying. 'They're from the Annoushka collection. Absolutely superb quality.' She says *Annoushka* like it's something magical.

'I love the pink …' the woman says. 'But let me try the green one.'

I figure it's all right if I just try the bracelet on. It's a little tricky to do up the clasp on my own but once it's on, I can't stop staring at my wrist. The bracelet is so beautiful. I twist my arm back and forth, watching the silver strands sparkle and gleam as they catch the light. I imagine myself showing it to Edi. 'I had to get one too!'

The customer has the green scarf on now. 'Gorgeous!' the shop assistant says. 'Perfect for your colouring.'

'I'm not so sure,' says the customer. 'Where's that blue one I tried on before?'

I lower my arm for a moment and my blazer sleeve slips down, covering the bracelet completely. You wouldn't even know I had it on. Suddenly I'm standing very still, holding my breath. Because a thought has just popped into my head. *What would happen if I walked out of the shop now?* The shop assistant has barely even noticed I'm here. I'm pretty sure she didn't see me try on the bracelet.

I'm going to do it. Not because I want to steal the bracelet – it's more like an experiment to see what happens.

If the shop assistant stops me I'll tell her that I forgot I had the bracelet on – just like I forgot about the mascara.

Taking the first step is hard, but each step after that is easier. Soon I'm level with the front counter. I feel my heart jump a little. Blood pumps loudly in my ears. 'Maybe the yellow?' the shop assistant is saying to the scarf lady. 'It's such a *now* colour.'

'It's too hard to choose!' sighs the customer. 'Maybe I should buy them all!' She and the shop assistant both laugh.

It's not until I step outside of the shop that I realise my hands are so tightly clenched they ache. I keep walking – fighting the urge to break into a run – and try to keep my breath as steady as I can. No-one stops me. The shop assistant doesn't even say goodbye. It's almost like I'm invisible. My legs are shaking like I've just run a marathon but I feel amazing. All tingly and super alive or something. I keep walking, away from the shop and towards the queue where I can see Dad waving to me like crazy from the front.

I run over to him and give him a bear hug. I can tell he's surprised, but also pleased. 'Feeling better?' he says, hugging me back.

'*So* much better,' I say. 'Oh, and Dad? You'll need 270 square metres of insulation for that job tomorrow.'

Dad grins and pulls some money out of his pocket. 'Go and get us some popcorn from the snack bar, kiddo,' he says. 'And some drinks.'

The movie is the most boring thing I've seen in my life, but it doesn't matter. I spend most of the time running my finger along the bracelet hidden under my sleeve. I can't believe how easy it was to make it mine.

Six

I wake up early the next morning on the inflatable mattress in Dad's new lounge room, which is also the dining room and kitchen. Carolyn is snoring away beside me on the couch. I lie there for a while, listening to the trucks rumbling past outside, with a funny feeling in my stomach – and I know it's because of the bracelet. Last night, taking the bracelet had felt exciting. But overnight the feeling has changed, like when you leave milk out of the fridge for too long and it goes all thick and lumpy.

I get up quietly and check the pocket of my school

uniform. It's where I hid the bracelet before going to bed last night. I think I'm hoping that maybe it's vanished or something. It hasn't, of course, but somehow it doesn't look quite so pretty anymore. *Maybe I should take it back,* I think. *Or give it away?* Then I hear Dad moving around in his room and I quickly zip the bracelet back into my pocket. I'll work out what to do with it later.

Mornings at Dad's place are always more relaxed than at Mum's. Dad doesn't hassle us about eating breakfast or worry about whether we're going to be late for school. He doesn't make us lunch either – just gives us some money for the canteen, which is fine by me.

I get ready quickly and don't bother about breakfast, because I want to catch the bus instead of waiting for a lift with Dad. I feel like I want to be on my own. The bus is pretty full, as usual, and even though it's stupid, I keep thinking that whenever anyone looks at me it's because they know what I did. That they can tell I nicked something.

When I get to school I head to the spot where Leni, Soph and I usually hang out before school starts – even though I know they won't be there yet.

I'm just rounding a corner near the lockers when I run into Ethan. Literally. I'm so shocked that I just stand there for a moment, gaping at him like an idiot. He's looking at me in the same way. Finally he says, 'I'd better go,' and tries to escape.

But I'm not having that. 'Are you going out with Hannah now?' I ask, blocking his way.

'No,' he says. 'We're just friends.'

'Oh yeah, *right*,' I say, super sarcastic. 'Just friends who hang out all the time and laugh and go and see weird old movies together.'

He gives me a strange look – probably because he doesn't realise I spotted him at the cinema last night. Then he says, 'Hannah likes weird old movies, just like I do. It's one of the reasons we're friends.'

'And what are the other reasons?' I say. 'It can't be that she's *pretty*.' I know that's a nasty thing to say. But I am getting mad. Ethan gets this really disgusted expression on his face and says, 'Maybe she's not as pretty as you, but she's smarter.'

I can't believe what I'm hearing! Ethan likes Hannah

better than me because she's *smarter?* What kind of guy *is* he? 'She is *not* smarter than me!' I manage to say eventually.

Ethan hesitates, like he's trying to decide if he should say something or not. He must decide not to, because he suddenly steps around me and starts heading off towards the library.

'You shouldn't have dumped me with a text message!' I yell after him. 'That's really rude, Ethan.'

He stops and turns back for a moment. 'You're right,' he says, in that calm way of his which is extremely annoying. 'That *was* rude and I'm sorry. But you know what, Anya? Sometimes it feels like the only way to get your attention is via your phone.' He walks away, totally taking advantage of the fact that I'm too gobsmacked to stop him.

Without even realising I'm doing it, I take the Cargo bracelet out of my pocket and put it on. The moment it's on, I feel better. More in control.

By the time Leni and Soph arrive, I'm not shocked anymore. Now I'm furious. 'Can you *believe* Ethan thinks Hannah is smarter than I am?' I say, fuming. I'm expecting them both to say, *That's crazy!* but they say nothing.

I narrow my eyes at them. 'You guys don't actually think that's true, do you?' I say.

'Well,' says Soph slowly, 'Hannah does always do pretty well in tests and stuff.'

'Especially in maths,' adds Leni. 'But you don't care, do you? You hate maths.'

The thing is, I didn't go to the same primary school as Leni or Soph, so they don't know that I used to be really good at maths. And it's not like I can suddenly say, *Actually I used to be a mathlete*, because how much of a loser would that make me look? There's only one thing I can do. I have to wait for a chance to show them – and Ethan – that I'm smarter than they think.

'Hey,' says Leni, pointing at my wrist. 'Pretty bracelet.' I know she's trying to change the topic, but she's right. The bracelet *is* pretty. It seems to have its sparkle back now that I'm outside.

'Thanks,' I say. 'My dad bought it for me. You know, to make me feel better about breaking up with Ethan.'

'Wow,' says Soph. 'That's so nice of him. It looks expensive.'

I shrug. 'Yeah, it probably is. But you can borrow it any time you like.'

V

In maths later that morning, Mr Cartright springs a surprise test on us. Everyone groans – except me, because I realise this is my chance to show everyone that they're wrong about me. That I *am* smart.

Just before the test starts, I see Hannah give Ethan a little smile and mouth the words *good luck* to him. It's totally sick-making.

Just you wait, I think to myself. *We'll see who's really smarter.*

V

The doctor's office is open late on Thursday evenings, so Mum isn't around for dinner. When my parents first split up, Carolyn and I used to make dinner together on Thursdays. Carolyn would do most of the cooking but I'd help a lot. It was actually pretty fun. But we haven't cooked together for ages and the moment I walk into the flat, I can tell that we won't be doing it this evening either. There's the sound of laughter and talking coming from Carolyn's room, which means that Max is over – even though he's not meant to visit during the week.

I check out the fridge and find some bread, a couple of soft-ish apples, some cheese and an old bunch of celery that's so limp that when I shake it, it looks like a big green hand, waving. I know how to cook pesto pasta on my own, but there are no jars of red pesto in the cupboard, so in the end I take the less-soft apple and a hunk of cheese and make myself some Vegemite toast. Then I sit down to eat it in front of the TV.

I can hear Max and Carolyn talking and laughing in her room. They've been going out for ages now. Maybe they'll get married one day. Will Carolyn ask me to be her bridesmaid? Last year I would've thought so, but now I'm not so sure. I just seem to bug her at the moment.

I don't know if it's because I'm sitting alone on our huge sofa, but I suddenly feel really small. Like I'm just this dot floating around in the universe, so tiny and unimportant that no-one even sees me. I curl up on the sofa and before I know it, I'm starting to drift off.

The next thing I know Mum's leaning over me, holding a box of what smells like Chinese takeaway. 'Hi, honey,' she says. 'Are you hungry? I've got you some chicken and vegies.' I sit up. The food smells good.

As I'm reaching out to take the container, Mum spots the bracelet on my arm. 'Where did *that* come from?' she asks.

'Dad gave it to me,' I say, because it's started to feel true.

Mum's face goes all tight. 'How lovely that someone's got money to fritter away,' she mutters.

The food smells bring Carolyn out of her room. Max doesn't appear so either she's stuffed him into a cupboard or he left while I was asleep.

'How's the homework going?' Mum asks.

Carolyn exhales loudly and plonks herself down on the sofa. 'I've been working at it solidly since I got home,' she says. Her eyes slide sideways, like she's daring me to contradict her.

Of course I wouldn't, but I can't resist teasing her a bit.

I pull this confused look and open my mouth like I'm about to say something. Then, when I see her panicked expression, I grin and shut my mouth again. When I go to my room later, I take the bracelet off and put it in the bottom of my schoolbag. I'm hoping that if Mum doesn't see it, she'll forget about it.

V

I'm just getting my lunch from my bag the next day when Mr Cartright comes up to me. He's looking very serious. I mean, he's not exactly Mr Jolly at the best of times, but today his face is even more stern than usual.

'Anya,' he says. 'Come to my office, please.'

What have I done? For once I don't have any make-up on, so it can't be that. I can see Leni and Soph looking at me wide-eyed. 'Now?' I say.

'Yes. Now.'

Mr Cartright shares an office with another teacher, but it's obvious which desk is his. It's the one with the three pens perfectly lined up beside a laptop, which is sitting open at exactly ninety degrees. Mr Cartright must have used a protractor to get the angle so straight. It's tempting to reach out while he's not looking and adjust the angle just the tiniest bit, to see how long it takes him to notice. But I don't.

Next to the laptop is a neatly stacked pile of tests. I take a peek – it's the one we did yesterday. Hannah's is sitting on the top. She got eighty-nine per cent. Mr Cartright takes the chair from the other desk and puts it down in front of me. 'Sit down please, Anya,' he says. The chair is way too high for me and my legs are dangling, but I don't want to try adjusting it in case I accidentally eject myself. I'm pretty sure Mr Cartright wouldn't find that funny.

Mr Cartright shuffles through the pile of tests, extracts one and places it in front of me. It's mine – and I got ninety-five per cent! *Ha!* I think. *Take that Hannah!*

'This is an excellent mark,' says Mr Cartright. It sounds like good news, but the tone of his voice tells me it's not. 'Anya,' he says. 'Did you cheat on this test?'

'No!' I say indignantly. 'I didn't!'

Mr Cartright silently turns his laptop around so the

screen is facing me. There's a spreadsheet open on it, with a list of all my marks for the year so far. Fifty-six per cent. Fifty-two per cent. Forty-nine per cent. Then right at the bottom there's my latest mark, in red. Ninety-five per cent.

'You can probably see why I'm a little suspicious,' Mr Cartright says quietly.

'I didn't cheat!' I say, hating the way my voice has suddenly gone all squeaky so I sound like I'm lying. 'I just tried really hard this time.' It's so, so unfair that when I actually do a good job, I still get into trouble.

Mr Cartright's eyebrows rise like two woolly sheep leaping into the air. 'Do you mean that you *didn't* try on all the other tests?' he says. 'You deliberately tried to get low marks?'

Okay, so I can see how that might sound strange – especially to someone like Mr Cartright. Because Mr Cartright is not a girl and if he was ever thirteen (which is hard to believe) it must have been a very long time ago. Too long ago for him to remember why someone might pretend not to be good at something. So I don't answer.

Mr Cartright leans forward, his hands clasped on the

desk in front of him. 'Anya, do you have any ideas about what you want to do when you leave school?' he asks me. I *hate* this question, but adults are obsessed with asking it. They're always going on about how you should enjoy being young, but they constantly ask you about what you'll do when you're old.

'No,' I mumble. 'Not yet.' I hope this will be enough, but it's not.

'Come on,' he says. 'You must have some idea.'

I fold my arms tightly. 'Well, nothing that's got anything to do with maths, that's for sure,' I say.

'Can I ask why?' Mr Cartright asks, and he looks genuinely surprised.

'Because maths is so boring!' I say.

I'm half-expecting Mr Cartright to lose it at me then. I get the feeling that he lives for maths. But instead he just does this long, drawn-out sigh and says, 'So, what then?'

'Maybe a buyer for a fashion label,' I say. I know this is Carolyn's dream, not mine, but I'm desperate and I'm hoping it'll shut him up because I'm pretty sure Mr Cartright will have no idea what a buyer is.

Luckily it seems to do the trick, because finally Mr Cartright pushes away from his desk and opens the office door. 'You can go for now,' he says.

The funny thing is that now I'm not sure I want to go. I don't know what he's thinking. I hover in the doorway. 'Mr Cartright? Do you believe me that I didn't cheat?' I ask.

He frowns at me in this puzzled way. 'I'm not sure yet,' he says. 'I'll have to think about it.'

'Oh,' I mutter. It's pretty hurtful to realise that Mr Cartright thinks I'm the sort of person who *might* cheat. But I guess it also means he thinks there's a chance that I didn't. I decide to risk asking one more question. 'What did Ethan get?' I ask.

'He got ninety-one per cent,' says Mr Cartright. 'You topped the class, Anya.'

It's amazing how good that makes me feel.

Seven

Mum is supposed to leave work early on Fridays, but the moment I step into the waiting room that afternoon, I know she's not going anywhere. It's like every sick person in the suburb has turned up. I hold my breath as I walk over to the desk to minimise the amount of germs I inhale.

'Sorry, honey,' says Mum. 'I'll be another hour.' She looks tired. Even more tired than usual. 'You can sit in the waiting room and do your homework if you want,' she suggests.

'That's okay,' I say quickly. 'I'll come back in an hour.'

There's no way I'm hanging around in here with all these sick people.

I pause at the top of the elevators, trying to decide what to do. I could catch a bus over to the cinema complex and take the bracelet back to Cargo, but the more I think about doing that, the more I realise how weird and awkward it would be. The woman in the shop might not believe I took it by accident. I could just try to sneak it onto a shelf somewhere, but I'd probably look pretty suss doing that. And that's when I have a brilliant idea. There's a charity bin not far from where I'm standing. I can put the bracelet in there and then I won't have to worry about it anymore. Plus giving stuff to charity is good, right?

I hurry over to the bin and take the bracelet out of my pocket, glancing around first to check that no-one is watching me. The flap of the charity bin creaks and clanks loudly as I pull it down. I put the bracelet on the chute then close it up. It feels good to hear the bracelet sliding away, deep down into the darkness. It's the sound of a problem being solved. I swear I feel a few kilos lighter as I walk back to the escalator.

Then I catch a glimpse of myself in a shop window and the heaviness returns. My chest is so *flat*. I look like a ten-year-old. So I decide to go visit the Charm Bra. Who knows? Maybe it's gone on sale or something.

When I get to the lingerie department, I can't find the Charm Bra anywhere. There are none left on the rack and I can't see them anywhere else in the teen section either. They must have sold them all. I feel completely gutted. The worst bit is knowing that there are a whole lot of other girls walking around in *my* bra, having their profiles boosted.

'Can I help you?' There's a shop assistant nearby, restocking. It's not the grandmothery lady from before. It's a girl who doesn't look all that much older than me and she's totally stylish. Everyone who works in the department store wears black – it must be their uniform – but unlike the other lady, who wore a boring black shirt and pants, this girl is wearing a really cute dress and shiny shoes. Pinned to her dress is her name badge, *Melissa*. Melissa has the best make-up on – it's sort of retro, I guess, with really thick eyeliner. I instantly decide I'm going to try to do mine like that, too.

Melissa smiles at me, not in a pushy shop-assistant way, but like she's being friendly. 'Can I help?'

'I was just wondering what happened to the purple bras which were hanging here a few days ago,' I say, pointing to the empty rack.

Melissa nods. 'The Charm Bras,' she says. 'They've been *really* popular.'

'So there's none left?' I say.

'There might be some out the back,' Melissa says. 'I'll go and check.' Her heels clack against the tiles as she walks off and I wait there, with all my fingers and even some of my toes crossed. A few minutes later she comes into view, holding up two Charm Bras triumphantly. 'It's your lucky day,' she says. 'These have literally *just* come in. They don't even have price tags on them yet.' Melissa hands them over to me. 'I think the 8B will probably be right for you, but they run a little large so I brought the 8A just in case.' I can't help grinning at that. She thinks I might be an 8B!

The material is even softer and silkier than I remember. 'It's a gorgeous bra, isn't it?' Melissa says. 'I've got one too.'

'It's the most beautiful bra ever,' I say.

'Go and try it on,' says Melissa. She feels more like my big sister than a shop assistant – except that she's way nicer to me than my real big sister is. 'I'll come and check on you in a few moments.'

V

The change room is completely deserted when I get there. There's no attendant waiting to give me a number, either. I hang by the entrance for a minute, waiting to see if anyone is going to turn up, but then I just go and choose a cubicle for myself.

I peel off my uniform and the boring white bra Mum bought me and dump them in the corner of the change room. I'm careful not to look at myself in the mirror at this stage – I don't want to catch a glimpse of that blue vein on my left boob. My hands are actually shaking a little from excitement as I put on the Charm Bra – the 8B, of course. The material feels really soft and nice against my skin and I manage to get it done up at the back without having to swivel it around to the front. Then I adjust the little buckles on the strap so that they're as short as possible. And it fits! Pretty much, at least – especially if I hold my shoulders right back.

I stand there for a few minutes, looking at my reflection, flipping my hair over my shoulder and smiling the way the model in the Charm Bra ad does. The change room has those adjustable mirrors so I can see how I look from the back and the side too. The bra looks great from every single angle. Then it's time for the big test. I grab my uniform from the corner and put it back on over the bra. Then I slip my jumper over the top of it and check out my reflection again. It's amazing – I look at least sixteen. And that's just while I'm wearing my baggy school uniform. I'd probably look even older if I was wearing something more body-hugging.

This feeling of longing swells up inside me then. I want the bra more than I've ever wanted anything in my whole life. Owning it will change everything for me. It'll change who I am and how people look at me. I just know that I'm meant to have it. But I also know there's no way Mum will ever buy it for me. And I can't wait the months and months it'd take me to save up for it. So I guess that's the end of the matter. I could cry.

Slowly I get undressed, take the bra off and put my old boring bra back on. Once I'm dressed again I unlock the change-room doors and start heading back into the shop. I spot Melissa over in Big Beige Land helping a customer. I guess that's why she never came to check on me.

I'm about to put the two bras on the table near the exit of the change rooms when I notice something. Not only do the bras have no price tags on them, but they also don't have any security tags. Which means there's nothing to set off the alarms if I were to walk out of the shop with them. I look at the bra, in all its shiny, purple loveliness. *I need this bra. I'm meant to have it.*

I step back into the change rooms and very slowly begin to unzip my bag. The noise sounds crazy loud to me – like thunder – but I keep going. When there's a big enough opening, I tuck the bra into my bag and quickly re-zip it. I leave the 8A on the change-room table, sling my bag on my shoulder and start walking towards the exit. It's funny –

I don't even feel nervous this time. I guess it's because the whole thing feels like fate. Maybe Melissa even wanted me to take the bra – that's why she gave me it to me without the security tag. There's terrible department-store muzak – 'Careless Whispers' – piping over the speakers and I hum along to it.

I feel a tiny bit nervous when I get to the scanners at the entrance to the store. It's dumb, but I'm still half-expecting the alarm to go off. It doesn't, though, and I walk out of the store and into the noise and smells of the food court. I realise I'm a little thirsty. Maybe I've got time to grab a Jokey Juice before I go up to meet Mum.

Then there's a hand on my arm, holding me back. 'Just a moment, please, young lady!' It's a security guard, dressed in department-store black. Standing beside him is Melissa. But she's not smiling at me now. Her face has gone really hard.

'Is this the girl?' the security guard asks her, and Melissa nods. The guard turns back to me. 'Unzip your bag, please,' he says.

When I felt his hand on my arm, it was like my heart

had stopped beating. But now it's making up for those lost moments by beating extra fast. 'Why?' I say. 'I left the bras back in the change room. If they're not there it's not *my* fault.' But neither of them seem to hear me. A group of girls walk past and stare curiously. My face burns.

I unzip my bag super slowly, hoping that maybe the bra will have worked its way down to the bottom of my bag where the guard won't see it. But it hasn't, and when I hold my bag open for the guard to see, it's sitting right up on the very top, the diamantés sparkling in the fluorescent lights of the food court. The only thing I feel glad about is that the bracelet isn't in there too.

A kid walks past with his mum. 'Look!' he says. 'That policeman's got that girl.' I keep my eyes down.

'I can't believe you did this,' says Melissa. She sounds disgusted. 'I did you a favour bringing out that bra with no security tags. I'll get into heaps of trouble thanks to you.'

A lump begins to form in my throat. 'I'm … I'm sorry,' I say.

Melissa rolls her eyes and doesn't even bother to reply. Instead she turns to the security guard. 'Can I go back to my department now?' she says. 'I need to make sure no more little girls are stealing bras that probably don't even fit them.'

Melissa is allowed to go. But I'm not. The security guard takes the bra out of my bag and tells me to follow him.

'Where are we going?' I say, panic starting to bubble up inside me.

'First stop is the security office,' the guard says.

I am way too scared to ask what the second stop will be.

Eight

As the guard leads me through the store I keep my eyes straight ahead, deliberately not looking at anyone, hoping no-one will guess what's going on. Maybe they'll think I work in the shop, or that I'm an undercover store detective. Or a lost kid.

We end up in the luggage department and the guard opens a door I've never noticed before. The office behind it is small and depressing. There are no windows, for one thing, and there's a pot plant that's all droopy and yellow. The only decoration on the walls is a bunch of *What to do in an emergency* posters – fire, flood, chemical spill.

There's a woman with short dark hair sitting at a desk, and she glances up as I walk in. She looks a little like the pot plant – as if she doesn't get enough sunlight. I guess that's not surprising if she spends all day in here.

'Shop theft,' the guard tells her, closing the door behind us.

The woman doesn't look shocked or even surprised. 'Sit there, please,' she says to me, pointing to a chair near the wall.

The security guard goes over to where a coffee machine is perched on a shelf and starts making himself a coffee. I'm dying for some water, but I don't want to ask.

The woman picks up the phone. 'How do I contact your parents?' she says.

It might sound dumb but up until this moment I hadn't really thought about that. About my parents finding out. They will freak. 'My parents have split up,' I say, trying to stall her. Maybe make her feel a little sorry for me too. It doesn't work.

'Well, who can get here first? Mum or Dad?' she says, a little impatiently. 'The sooner someone comes, the sooner we can get through this.'

My mouth has gone all dry. Mum and Dad are both going to hit the roof so hard their heads will leave permanent dents in the ceiling. I think about getting them to call Carolyn, but she's at her friend Lucia's place this afternoon and she'd probably be cross at me for calling her. Plus I'm pretty sure that a big sister wouldn't count for this woman anyway.

'Mum works here in the mall. In the doctor's office on level five,' I say in the end. I feel sick. Dizzy too. Maybe I'll vomit or pass out and they'll have to take me to hospital. Then they'll discover the blue vein and they'll realise that I'm actually dying or something. 'She's one of the receptionists,' I manage to add.

The woman nods. 'Dr Walters' office, right?' she says and dials the number without me having to give it to her. It'd be just my luck that this woman turns out to be one of Shelley's patients. As it's ringing, she says, 'What's your mum's name?'

'Jillian Saunders,' I croak. Then I shake my head. 'I mean, Jillian *Hoffman*.'

The woman looks at me suspiciously – like maybe

I'm trying to pull something here – but before she can say anything someone picks up the phone at the other end and I faintly hear my mum's voice saying, *Dr Walters' office, how may I help you?'*

'Mrs Hoffman?' says the woman. Her voice is all brisk and no-nonsense, like she's made this call hundreds of times before. Maybe she has. 'This is Rachel White. I'm calling from Westland Mall security. We have your daughter –' She stops and looks at me with raised eyebrows and I can see I'm meant to fill in my name.

'Anya,' I mutter.

The woman's eyes flick away from me again. 'We have Anya here. I'm afraid she's been caught shoplifting. We need you to come to the office immediately so we can discuss the next step.'

I scrunch down into my chair, trying not to overhear what Mum is saying on the other end of the phone. The woman tells Mum where to find us and the phone clicks back into its cradle. 'She's coming,' she says to me and then starts tapping away at her computer, completely ignoring me.

It probably only takes Mum about five minutes to

arrive, but it feels like the longest wait of my life. When she finally pushes through the door her face is all flushed and sweaty like she ran here. Her hair is coming unpinned at the front and she still has her name badge on her cardigan.

The security woman stands up and introduces herself. 'I'm Rachel White,' she says. 'And this is Joe, our security guard. Sorry for calling you at work, Mrs Hoffman.'

'It's *Ms* Hoffman,' Mum says. Then she looks over at me. 'Are you okay?' she says, and her strange calmness freaks me out. I was expecting her to start telling me off the moment she walked in here.

I nod. 'Yeah, I'm okay.'

Joe gets a chair for Mum and a glass of water. Everything feels so weird. As if we're all pretending this is somehow *normal* when really, not one thing about it is normal. Not being in this nasty little office hidden behind a wall. Not Mum and I sitting down when we should be in the car, singing loudly to the radio as we drive home. It's all making me nervous. I wish I could give Mum a hug or, even better, have her give me one. But it's like we're both frozen into our seats.

'I'm sorry, Mum,' I say, trying to break the spell.

Joe jumps on that. 'You should be,' he says. 'I bet this is the last thing your mum needs.'

'Yes,' says Mum, quietly. 'It is. It really, really is.' She takes a sip of water and when she speaks again, her voice is louder. And harder. 'So, what did my daughter supposedly take?'

The word *supposedly* makes my heart leap a little with hope. Maybe she doesn't believe I actually stole anything! Maybe she's going to argue our way out of here! She's done something like that before. Back at primary school, someone scribbled all over our classroom wall with a permanent pen. Someone said *I* did it, and I got in trouble even though it wasn't me at all. I came home crying like anything, and the next morning Mum marched into school and told my teacher that she knew I hadn't done it because I wasn't *that sort of kid*.

'I found this in her bag,' says Joe and he holds up the bra. I feel like I want to die when I see the look on Mum's face.

'Oh, Anya,' she says. 'I can't believe it.' The worst bit is her thinking that maybe I *am* that sort of kid after all.

Then there are a whole lot of questions about my full name and address and birth date, which Rachel types straight into the computer. Then she picks up the bra and examines it carefully. 'Well, we certainly won't be able to sell it now,' she states. 'It's ruined.'

'What do you mean?' Mum says.

Rachel holds the bra out to Mum and points to a bluey-purple blotch on one of the cups. 'It looks like ink.'

Mum takes the bra and touches the blotch. Sure enough, some of the blue colour comes away on her fingertip. I know straight away what it must be – the same stupid pen at the bottom of my bag that leaked all over my muesli bar.

'It'll have to be paid for,' Rachel says.

'Right now?' says Mum.

'That would be best,' says Rachel. 'It's $89.95.'

I see Mum bite the corner of her mouth but she doesn't say anything. She seems numb. And her numbness is spreading to me too, like it's contagious. Mum's hand fumbles as she pulls her purse out of her bag. 'I can take credit card,' says the woman, like this is just any normal sale.

Mum shakes her head. 'No, I think I've got enough

in cash.' We all watch as she starting pulling out notes, one after another. It's painfully slow. Then, when she's pulled out all her notes, she opens up the coin pocket and starts making piles of coins on Rachel's desk, beside the notes. When she's finally got enough, her purse is almost completely flat. I wish I had some money to give her. But I've got nothing.

Rachel produces a little metal cashbox and puts all of Mum's money into it. Then the box is locked with a key. Rachel writes out a receipt and hands it to Mum, along with the bra. Mum pushes them both into her bag.

'I'll pay you back,' I whisper to her.

'Yes,' says Mum, in this really cold way. 'You certainly will.'

'So,' says Rachel briskly. 'Now it's time to call the police.'

I hear myself yelp. I'm so shocked that I actually jump up from my chair and I hear it fall over behind me. 'No, don't!' I say. Everyone stares at me. 'Aren't you just going to tell me off or something? Give me a warning?'

Joe suddenly gets really mean. 'Young lady – do you think this is a game?' he snaps at me. 'You're in a lot of trouble. You might think you're just a kid and that you can get away with stealing stuff, but this store takes theft very seriously. When we catch a thief like you – no matter what age – it's store policy to call the police.'

A thief! He called me a thief! Straight away, I picture the warning sign in the cinema toilets with that shadowy hand pinching someone's purse. Is that what I am? It's not how I think of myself – and it's horrible to have other people thinking of me this way. I'm a good person! My chest feels tight and I'm too shocked to say anything so I just look down. One of the leaves from the pot plant has fallen off and I find myself staring at it. It looks just like how I'm feeling inside. All twisted up.

'Is it really necessary to call the police?' says Mum. 'It's the first time she's done anything like this, after all.' Her voice sounds pretty calm but I can tell she's worried, which makes me feel more scared than ever.

'Perhaps it's the first time she's been *caught* stealing,' Rachel says grimly, 'but we generally find that shoplifters have stolen a number of smaller items before they get sloppy enough to be caught.'

I feel my face go hot, thinking about the bracelet.

'I can guarantee Anya won't do anything like this again,' says my mum. 'She won't be able to, because I won't be letting her out of my sight until she's twenty-five.'

Rachel and Joe look at each other for what feels like forever, and then finally Rachel leans back in her chair and sighs loudly. 'Look,' she says to Mum. Her voice has changed a little. She sounds less official. More like a real person. 'I wouldn't normally do this, but because you work in the complex, and as the goods have now been paid for, I'm prepared to be more lenient than usual.'

Mum starts to gush gratitude, but Rachel puts her hand up to stop her. 'There are some conditions, though. Anya will have to sign a statement admitting that she stole these goods, and she will be banned from entering this store for twelve months.'

Joe jabs his finger at me. 'And don't think you can just sneak back in, young lady,' he says, 'because I will recognise you.'

'If we catch her here, she will be forcibly removed or charged with trespassing. And if she's caught stealing from us again,' continues Rachel, 'we will be pressing charges.'

'Thanks,' says Mum, rising to her feet. 'Thank you both so, so much.' Then she grabs my arm and starts leading me towards the door. When I say *leading*, I mean *pulling*. 'I promise this won't happen again,' she calls over her shoulder. Then we rush out before they have a chance to change their minds.

I have never been so glad to leave a room in my life.

The store is closing up when we get out. Roller shutters are rattling down into position and staff members are having their bags checked as they leave the shop. Mum walks so quickly towards the exit that I have to jog to keep up with her. She winds her way through the displays and then out into the underground car park. Her lips are tightly pressed together and her face is hard and unreadable. It's not until we're both sitting in the car that she puts her head on the steering wheel and starts crying.

Seeing Mum cry makes me feel like a terrible person – the worst – but I don't know what to say or do to make her stop. I actually wish I could cry too, but I feel like there's something plugging up the tears, stopping them from coming. All I can do is sit there in the passenger seat and listen to my mum cry.

'I feel so humiliated,' she sobs. 'Having those two looking at me like I'm a terrible mother. Like I don't know how to raise my kids properly.'

'You're not a terrible mother,' I say. 'You're an awesome mum.' But for some reason this just makes her cry even more.

It takes a while, but Mum's crying gets less intense and finally she sits up and pulls her phone out of her pocket. Her expression has changed again. She's got her *don't try to talk me out of this* face on.

'Who are you calling?' I ask nervously.

'Your father,' Mum says, with the phone already positioned at her ear. 'He needs to know about this.'

If you ask me, there's no reason for Dad to know anything, but a moment later he answers and Mum gives him the run-down on what happened. I'm hoping this will be it, but that's wishful thinking. Dad wants to see me immediately and a few minutes later we're heading for our old house to meet him.

Nine

You can tell by looking at our place that no-one's living in it. It's not just the piles of junk mail bursting out of the letterbox or the grass being a bit too long. It just *looks* empty, somehow. Dad's van is parked out the front and I can see him sitting in it, smoking a cigarette. That's not a good sign. Dad only smokes when he's mad or upset. He gets out and crushes the cigarette on the road when we pull up.

Mum and Dad start up their usual routine before we've even gone through the front door.

'You sure took your time getting here,' Dad says.

'So it's my fault that the traffic was bad?' Mum says.

'I bet you took Glenburn Road,' says Dad. 'Even though I've told you a thousand times that Wendall Road is faster.'

'No, it's not,' Mum says. 'Glenburn is the quickest way.' They argue about roads for a while and then the topic switches.

'Why was Anya wandering around Westland Mall on her own, anyway?' Dad asks.

'Because I have to work, Steve,' Mum snaps back. 'And I thought I could trust her on her own for an hour.' Then they both look at me like they're thinking, *Well, that's obviously not the case.*

As we walk inside, Dad launches into the lecture I knew would be coming. About how disgusted he is with me. How disappointed. But I'm finding it hard to concentrate. I haven't been to the house for a few weeks and it's weird how different it feels. It's all echoey for one thing, and it feels much bigger than it did when we were in it – like the emptiness has pushed the walls further apart. It stinks of fresh paint too.

'You've really let me down, Anya,' Dad says as we all troop into the lounge room.

I *am* listening (it's impossible not to) but I'm also trying to work out what's missing from the room. I mean, obviously there are a *lot* of things missing. All the pictures are gone and pretty much all of the furniture. All that's left are two armchairs, which have been pushed into the centre of the room and covered with white sheets. They look like ghosts – short fat ones. The painters covered them to stop them getting paint-splattered, I guess. But the thing that's missing isn't the furniture or pictures. It's something else. I just can't work out what it is right now.

Mum is frowning at the two chairs. 'Why are those still here?' she says.

Dad groans and plonks himself down on one. 'I don't know where you expect me to take them, Jill,' he says. 'My place is the size of a cupboard.' He sits up. 'Anyway, we're not here to talk about chairs.' He's looking at me as he says it. 'So, what did you take?' he asks.

I really, *really* don't want him to know – it's way too embarrassing – but Mum fishes the bra out of her bag and hands it to him. It's all squashed out of shape now, as well as being ink-stained, and I can tell that Dad isn't really sure what it is at first. And when he does work it out, he's even more puzzled.

'What did you take *this* for?' he asks. I just shrug and look at the ground. How can I explain to him about wanting to *boost my profile* and about how good it felt when I was wearing that bra? How it helped me feel better about the whole Ethan thing and forget about that scary blue vein. Dad wouldn't get it. He'd probably just tell me the story – the one I've heard a thousand times already – about how he worked two jobs for three years so he could afford his first van.

Dad dumps the bra on the arm of the chair. 'What's her punishment going to be?' he asks Mum.

'Well, she's going to be working off the money she owes me by helping out in the doctor's office,' says Mum. This is the first I've heard of it. Mum must have come up with this plan during our long, silent drive home.

'How long do I have to do that for?' I ask, and instantly realise I've made a mistake. Mum whirls around and glares at me.

'For as long as it takes me not to be angry, Anya.'

Judging from her face right now, that could be a while.

Frankly, I think this is a massive punishment, but it's not enough for my parents. They become almost civilised as they talk about how else to punish me.

'What about no movie nights with her friends for a month?' suggests Mum.

'Two months,' says Dad. 'And no pocket money for three.'

I keep waiting for them to remember the school social, because the moment they do they'll ban me from going. But neither of them mentions it. 'There needs to be something else,' Dad keeps saying. 'One more thing.'

In the end I can't stand it anymore. 'The school social,' I blurt out. 'You're supposed to ban me from that.'

They both look at me in surprise. 'Don't you want to go?' asks Mum.

'Yes, I want to go,' I say, a little sulkily.

'So why did you suggest it?' asks Dad suspiciously.

I sigh and flop into one of the ghost chairs. 'Because I knew you'd remember it in the end and I want to get this over and done with.'

My parents agree that I can't go to the social, and I think that maybe we're finally done when Mum says something that makes everything way, way worse. 'And how about you rein in the gift-giving too,' she says to Dad. 'No more expensive jewellery for a while, okay?'

Dad looks astonished and straight away I know this won't be good. 'What?' he says.

Mum rolls her eyes. 'You know. The silver bracelet you gave Anya a few days ago.'

'I have no idea what you're talking about,' says Dad.

And then they both look at me, and Mum says, 'Anya?' So I have to tell them about the bracelet. And even though I explain that I put it in the charity bin (which you would think they'd be happy about), I'm now in so much trouble that basically my life is over.

For some reason, it's then that I finally realise what's missing from the room. The pencil lines in the doorframe. The ones that Dad made to measure our heights on each birthday. The doorframe is now shiny, clean and white. I jump up and run over to examine it, and there's already a lump forming in my throat. Even up close, there's no sign of the lines. No-one would know they'd ever been there at all.

'They're gone!' I say, and there's a wobble in my voice. 'Our heights. You let the painters paint over the top of them.'

Mum and Dad stare at me for a moment. 'Well, we had to,' Mum says eventually. 'The person who buys the house won't be interested in how tall you girls were when you were five. You didn't really think we'd leave it, did you?'

It's funny the things that make you cry and the things that don't. I didn't cry when my parents told us they were splitting up. I didn't cry when they announced they were selling the house. And even today, when I was caught by the security guard, I didn't cry. But for some reason, knowing those pencil lines have been erased forever makes me burst into tears. 'I knew the new owner would paint over them in the end,' I sob. 'I just didn't think you guys would do it for them.'

I run back over to a ghost chair and curl up into it. Mum comes over and sits on one arm, and after a while I hear Dad sit on the other. Neither of them say anything. They just let me cry.

'It's really happening, isn't it?' I say. 'The house is going to be sold. We'll never live here again.' I feel like my past is being painted over, along with those pencil lines.

Dad's hand starts to stroke my back, just like he did when I was a little kid having trouble getting to sleep. 'Ah, kiddo,' he says softly. 'Change is tough, isn't it?'

Yeah, it's tough. And these two haven't made it any easier. Suddenly I'm mad – *really* mad – at them. I sit up. 'You guys shouldn't fight so much,' I say. 'It's really embarrassing when you shout at each other over the phone when we're out in public.'

Mum looks shocked. 'We don't do that, do we?'

'Yeah, you do,' I say. 'All the time! I *hate* it. And you shouldn't say mean things about each other to me. It makes me feel like you want me to take sides.'

They both go really quiet then and it's obvious they're shocked. Finally Mum says, 'Like your dad said, things are changing a lot at the moment. And we're at a really difficult, stressful point right now. But this is the worst bit. After the house is sold, things will get better, I promise.'

But I can't be talked around that easily. 'How can you

promise that?' I say. 'You don't know for sure that things will get better. They might get worse.'

'Well, we'll just have to make sure of it,' Mum replies. I want to believe her, but I'm not sure that I do.

Then Dad makes a suggestion – one that really surprises me, and I can tell it surprises Mum too. 'Maybe we need some help with all of this,' he says. 'Not with staying together,' he adds quickly, although he doesn't really need to. We all know there's no way that's going to happen. 'But help with splitting apart. You know – developing an exit plan or something.'

Mum nods. 'Yes,' she says. 'That's a good idea. I'll ask Shelley if she can recommend anyone.'

Things kind of calm down a little after that. Dad grabs his toolbox from his van and does a couple of repair jobs that Mum's been pestering him about for ages. Mum cleans the downstairs windows.

I go upstairs to my old bedroom to check if anything's been left behind. The door of the built-in wardrobe is open and I have this sudden memory of how I played in there with a torch as a little kid, pretending it was a cave and I was an explorer. Taking my keys from my pocket, I climb inside the cupboard and scratch some words into the wood, right at the back. *Anya Saunders was here.* Maybe some kid will find it one day. I guess it's a kind of dumb thing to do, but it makes me feel better somehow.

Then Dad phones for pizza and we end up eating it on the lounge-room floor. I can tell they've been talking while I was upstairs because halfway through dinner, Mum says, 'Now, Anya, your dad is going to pay for the bracelet you took and that's going to count as your birthday present from him this year. Does that sound fair?' It sounds totally *terrible* to me, but naturally I don't say that. Besides, I know my dad and he'll find it almost impossible not to buy me something for my birthday. But I don't say that either. I just nod.

Then Mum takes my hand and gives it a squeeze. 'Anya,' she says, and her voice is very soft now. 'We're really sorry about how things have been recently. We forgot what this break-up is like for you and Carolyn. Your dad and I have agreed that we'll try to do better.'

Then Dad joins in. 'But kiddo, you've got to promise

us something too.' I know what's coming, of course, but I let him say it anyway. 'We'd like you to promise us that you'll never do anything like this again. No more stealing.'

I say that I won't and they both seem satisfied. But I wish there was some way that I could really prove to them just how truly I mean it. How I know that I absolutely won't ever do anything like this again. I never want to feel like I did in that security office again. But I guess the only way I can show them is over time. Which sucks, because I hate waiting.

We eat the rest of our pizza in silence. But it's one of those good silences. As we're finishing up, Dad says, 'This is a good house, isn't it?'

Mum nods. 'I bet whoever buys it will be happy here.' And for the first time, instead of feeling jealous of someone else getting our house, I feel good thinking that maybe they'll love it as much as I did.

When it's time to go, we all leave the house and Mum locks up. I wonder to myself if this is the last time I'll go inside, and what it'll be like to drive past when there's another family living in there, playing in our backyard, marking their own heights on the doorframes. Maybe it won't be so bad. It'd have to be better than seeing the place look all sad and empty like this.

Dad goes around to the back of his van, opens it and slides in his toolkit. Then he pulls out a cardboard box and comes over to hand it to Mum. It's the missing iron.

'Took this by mistake,' he says with a sheepish grin. 'Thought it was my old sandwich toaster.' He kisses the top of my head goodbye. 'See you on Wednesday, kiddo,' he says.

As he drives off, Mum puts her arm around me and hugs me close to her side. We wave until he's out of sight.

Ten

I have a quiet weekend – basically I have no life now that I'm being punished. Leni calls to invite me over for a DVD night but I make an excuse. I've decided not to tell my friends about the whole shoplifting thing. Not yet, anyway. Luckily I'm good at hiding my emotions. I just act super bouncy and no-one has any idea how I'm actually feeling.

We have maths first thing on Monday morning, and as we're heading for the classroom my stomach starts doing little flips. Mr Cartright hasn't said anything to me yet about the maths test but I figure today will be the day. What will happen? With the way my luck is going he's probably decided to have me expelled, or at least suspended. Just imagine how overjoyed my parents would be about *that*.

So I spend the entire lesson stressing about it, but it's not until the end that Mr Cartright finally hands out our tests. My heart is thumping as I take mine. I'm half-expecting to see that ninety-five per cent crossed out. But it's still there and Mr Cartright even smiles at me. At least, I think that's what he's trying to do. 'Well done,' he says.

Leni leans over to see. 'Whoa, Anya!' she says in her foghorn voice. 'That's such an amazing mark!'

I feel all the blood rush to my face as everyone else turns around, trying to see what I got. 'It was just a fluke,' I mutter.

Mr Cartright turns back around then and gives me a funny look. 'Anya got the top mark on this test,' he announces. 'Which just shows what you can do if you put in a little effort.'

The bell goes and I'm just about to walk out when Mr Cartright stops me. 'I'd like a quick word, please.'

My stomach turns over. 'I'll catch up with you guys,'

I call to Leni and Soph, and they nod and shoot me sympathetic looks.

'So,' says Mr Cartright when everyone's gone. 'You'll be glad to know that I believe you didn't cheat. That's good, isn't it?'

I nod, but there's something about Mr Cartright's voice that makes me think there's more to come. Something I might not like.

'Do you want to know why?' he asks, and without waiting for an answer he produces a computer print-out from a stack of papers on his desk. My insides lurch sideways as I take in the picture. It's a frizzy-haired girl wearing a baggy, cacky-brown uniform, holding up a bunch of cardboard medals and grinning like an idiot. Along the bottom is written, *Mathlete of the Year!*

I want to snatch that piece of paper and rip it into a thousand pieces. 'Where did you get that?'

'Your old teacher, Miss Smith, emailed it to me,' says Mr Cartright calmly. 'I rang up your primary school after our chat on Friday. Miss Smith was more than happy to tell me about what a great student you were. In fact, she raved to me about how gifted you were in maths.'

It feels like a pretty sneaky thing for Mr Cartright to do – ringing my old school like that. But Mr Cartright doesn't look ashamed. He's looking pretty proud of himself, actually. He leans back in his chair and locks his hands across his chest.

'Things are going to change from now on, Anya,' he says. 'There'll be no more pretending you don't *get it*. No more just scraping by in tests. And no brushing your good marks off as *flukes*.' He puts a few sheets of paper down in front of me, covered with maths problems. 'I'm going to start giving you extra homework too and there's also a form for an upcoming maths competition that –'

'I'm not entering any maths competitions,' I say firmly, cutting him off. 'Or doing extra work. I won't deliberately do badly anymore, but I'm not doing anything else.' There's no way I'm letting him turn me into a *favourite*.

'That's ridiculous,' snaps Mr Cartright. 'I'm not letting this go.'

But I'm not backing down either. There's a moment when we just glare at each other. And then I have an idea.

One of those ideas that appear when you're desperate. 'What if I come up with some kind of extra maths thing on my own?' I say. 'Like, a project or something?' I'm not really sure what I mean – maybe helping Dad with his insulation stuff – but I basically just want Mr Cartright to get off my case. And I definitely don't want him enrolling me in maths competitions. I can tell he thinks I'm trying to get out of it but finally he says, 'Well, you come up with some ideas and we'll discuss it.'

He lets me go, but just as I'm opening the door he calls me again. 'If you don't come up with an alternative project, you *will* be enrolled in the maths competition, okay?'

I don't doubt for a second that he means it too.

V

When I finally meet up with my friends they are discussing the social, which is only five days away now. 'Mum says we can all meet at my house,' says Leni, 'and she'll drive us there together.' I don't want to talk about the social, but at some stage I'll have to break the news that I won't be there.

'Actually, I'm not going now after all,' I say, shrugging like the whole thing is no big deal.

'Oh no!' says Leni.

'Why?' says Soph. 'Is this because of Ethan again?'

'No, it's not because of him,' I say quickly. 'I just don't want to go because I know it will be completely lame. I'm actually pretty surprised that *you* guys want to go.'

Then Soph looks at me in that way she does. Like she's a bloodhound, sniffing out clues. 'What's going on, Anya? You've been acting really weird.'

'No, I haven't!' I say.

'Yes, you have,' corrects Soph. 'You've been doing that super-chirpy thing that you always do when you're upset but don't want to tell us why.'

The *good* thing about friends is that they know how you're feeling, no matter how hard you try to hide it. The *bad* thing is that you can't get away with anything! I flop down onto the grass and close my eyes, because then I can't see my friends' faces when they find out what a bad person I am. A *thief.*

'I'm not going because I'm not *allowed* to go, all right?

I'm not allowed to do anything – no movies, no shopping trips. Nothing for at least two months. Which is just as well because Mum and Dad cut off my allowance anyway.'

Leni and Soph are both quiet for a minute, letting this all soak in.

'What happened?' asks Leni, and her voice is full of concern. Then she squishes up next to me on the grass. 'Go on,' she says. 'Tell us.'

When I don't answer, Soph squishes up on my other side so it's like I'm trapped in a sandwich. A *friend*wich, I guess.

So I tell them. The whole story. All about the Charm Bra and how it felt like I was meant to have it, but I didn't have enough money. And then about the shoplifting stuff and all about being caught and how bad it made me feel when Mum was so upset. My friends listen in the way I like people to listen – without making any shocked noises or interrupting or anything. Just *listening*. But because I've got my eyes shut, I've got no idea what they think about all this. Whether they're shocked or they hate my guts or whatever.

When I've finished, I feel two opposite things at once. I'm relieved that it's out there, but I'm also really, really scared about what my friends will say. So I say something first. 'I guess you must think I'm a terrible person now, huh?'

I feel Leni sit up and I open my eyes. She doesn't look like she hates me, but she does look serious. 'Anya Saunders,' she says. 'You are so *not* a terrible person. You are one of the most generous people I've ever met. You're always lending out your stuff, or giving it away.'

Then Soph joins in. 'Leni's right,' she says. 'And you always help out with stuff too – like when you came on that "March for the Forests" with me and Mum last month. I know you didn't really want to go, but you did it anyway. That meant a lot.'

I feel my eyes starting to go all blurry. 'So you guys don't think I'm some manky thief?' I say, my voice catching in my throat.

Leni bear-hugs me. 'No way! You're Anya the Amazing,' she says.

Soph nods. 'So you made a dumb mistake,' she says. 'Everyone does that.' Then she places her hand across her chest and presses it. 'But you're good in here, you know?'

I'm seriously close to losing it now. 'Gee thanks, guys, for making me cry,' I say, trying to make a joke of it. But the thing is that even though I'm teary, I feel lighter. Like my friends' words have lifted me up. Given me a boost.

'If you're not going to the social, then I'm not going either,' Leni declares suddenly.

Soph nods in agreement. 'We'll just come around to your place and watch a DVD instead.'

This shocks me out of crying. 'No!' I say. 'You guys *have* to go. I'm not allowed to have DVD nights anyway, remember? I want you to go and tell me what it's like.' I don't tell them that I'm actually hoping they'll finally meet some guys they like, and my triple-dating dreams will come true.

My friends still look unsure. '*Please* go,' I say. 'I need you to be there. Because if you see Ethan slow-dancing with Hannah you have to jump in between them, okay?' In the end they laugh and say that they'll go after all. Just for me.

Eleven

Working at the doctor's clinic turns out to be not as bad as I was expecting. I don't have to deal with the patients, which is a big relief. There's a little room out the back where all the files and stuff are kept. On my first afternoon there, Mum handed me a huge stack of medical journals. 'These all need to be filed,' she told me. And basically that's what I've been doing every day. It's not just as simple as bunging them in on a shelf, either – I have to look through them all to see if there are any articles that might be useful for Shelley. Mum said to mark anything that's about old people, young mothers or teenagers, as these are the people who come to our clinic the most. I have to mark anything good with a Post-it note and leave it for Shelley to read.

I find the journals kind of fascinating. I mean, some of the images are really gross, but it's almost hard to look away. And the articles about teenagers are actually pretty interesting.

One afternoon, as I'm flipping through a journal, I come to an article called *Teen Concern: Breast Abnormalities*. It's all about how teenage girls worry a lot about whether what's happening to their bodies is the same as what's happening to everyone else. It says that teenagers are often too embarrassed or too worried to talk to anyone about it. The article has some examples and when I read example number three, my heart practically stops. One of the patients the doctor had seen was a girl who was convinced there was something wrong with her because she'd found a blue vein on her left breast! The doctor reassured her patient that this was totally normal, and told her all about the different ways breasts could look as they were developing. The article describes how her patient had burst into tears because she was so relieved. The funny thing is that reading this, I feel like bursting into tears myself.

It's weird to think of someone else worrying about exactly the same thing as me. It's good in a way, I guess, but it also makes me feel dumb for not talking to someone about it before – it would've saved me a whole lot of worry.

I am so engrossed in reading that I don't hear Shelley come in. She glances over my shoulder. 'That looks interesting,' she says.

'Yeah,' I say. 'It is.' I feel a bit embarrassed because she's caught me reading about *breast abnormalities,* but since she's already seen it I work up the guts to ask her something. 'There's a girl in here who saw her doctor because she was worried something was wrong with her, but it turns out she's fine. Does that happen a lot?' I say it very casually so Shelley won't guess it's got anything to do with me.

'All the time,' says Shelley, pouring herself a glass of water at the sink.

'And do you get annoyed with people like that – for wasting your time?' I ask.

Shelley looks at me in surprise. 'Of course not!' she says.

'It's always good to be able to tell someone that everything's fine. It's much better when people feel they can come to me with their worries, rather than stressing about it in private.'

I close the journal, while Shelley drinks her water.

'It must be good,' I find myself saying. 'Helping people the way you do.' Up to this point I figured being a doctor was mostly about trying not to be sneezed on. But it would be great to know everything Shelley knows about the body – to understand what is or isn't concerning, and know how to treat any problems.

'It *is* good,' agrees Shelley. 'And interesting.' Then she smiles at me. 'I know we joke about it, but have you ever actually thought about becoming a doctor yourself? I think you'd make a good one.'

I shrug. 'Well, maybe,' I say. And for the first time in a long time, I'm semi-serious about it.

I end up catching the bus home on my own that evening because Mum is working late. Carolyn's door is closed which makes me wonder if Max is in there. I go to the kitchen and pour myself some orange juice. It's only when I'm heading back to my room that I hear a weird noise coming from Carolyn's room. It sounds like crying.

I sneak up closer and press my ear against her door. Yep, someone is definitely crying in there. But it's not like there's anything I can do about it. When Carolyn's door is closed, I'm not welcome in her room. I'm not really welcome in there when it's *open* either. I sneak back to my room and try to get started on my homework.

But the noise of Carolyn's crying comes right through the wall and it's not showing any sign of stopping. It's pretty distracting. Eventually I put down my pen, go back down the hall and fling open Carolyn's door. I do it fast so there's no time to chicken out.

Carolyn is sprawled face-down on her bed. She looks up at me and her face is all red and blotchy.

'What's wrong?' I say.

Carolyn buries her face into her pillow. 'Go away,' she says in this muffled voice.

I start feeling cross. I mean, if anyone should be crying,

it's me. I'm the one who got busted shoplifting. I'm the one who was dumped for not being *smart enough*. And I'm the one who doesn't get to go to the school social. But I'm not blubbering away in my room, am I?

Being cross makes me braver. 'I'm not going anywhere,' I say, folding my arms. 'Not until you tell me what you're crying about.'

Carolyn sits up, and for a moment I think she's about to blast me. But then she kind of *crumples*. She puts her hands over her face and says something that sounds like, 'Max broke up with me.' Except it can't be that.

'What did you say?' I ask, taking a step closer.

Carolyn takes her hands away, and this time when she speaks there's no chance I've heard it, wrong. 'Max broke up with me. This afternoon. He said I was getting *too serious*.'

For a minute I just stand there, with my mouth hanging open. I never *ever* thought Carolyn and Max would split up. I thought they'd be together forever. 'Oh,' I say. 'That's … terrible.'

And then Carolyn starts crying even harder than before. She turns into a crying fountain, spouting tears in every direction. Because I'm not sure what else to do, I go and sit next to her, all the time waiting for her to yell at me to get out of her room. But she doesn't. Then I even work up enough courage to put my arm around her for a hug. I can't remember the last time Carolyn let me get this close, let alone let me hug her. Not since before Dad left, I think. I sit there for a while, trying to think of something to say that will cheer her up. But what can I possibly say?

After a few minutes, the crying eases off a bit and then eventually stops, although her breath is still all hiccuppy. She gives me a watery smile and says, 'Thanks for not trying to cheer me up.'

I shrug, like this was what I'd meant to do all along, and say, 'I know how it feels, being dumped.'

It's a bit risky saying this, because lately Carolyn hasn't liked me comparing anything in her life with my own. But this time she doesn't give me her usual death stare. Instead, she sighs and says, 'It sucks, doesn't it?' Like we're equals for once. And then she blurts something else out too. 'Max isn't the only reason why I'm upset, though. I'm failing maths. Like, *really* failing.'

'I bet you wouldn't fail if you tried harder,' I say.

But Carolyn shakes her head. 'No,' she says. 'I *have* tried. I've tried really hard. We're doing algebra at the moment and I just don't get it at all. I'm too dumb.'

Carolyn is in the bottom stream for maths. *Vegie* maths, some kids call it. I don't know what happens if you fail vegie maths. Do you get held back a year? Kicked out of school?

'Well, you already know you want to be a buyer,' I say. 'You won't need maths for that, will you?'

To my horror, Carolyn starts crying again. 'I do need maths for that. The buyer for Tude told me it's really important. She said you have to be able to stick to a budget and do quick calculations and currency conversions all the time. I'm hopeless at that sort of stuff. She said it's essential that I keep up my maths for as long as I can – but I don't think I'm going to make it through this term, let alone the rest of high school.'

'I'll help you,' I say. The words come out before I've really thought them through. Carolyn is three years above me. Will I really be able to help? 'I mean, we might be able to figure out your algebra stuff together.'

At first, Carolyn says no way and that it won't work. But the more I think about it, the more I'm sure that I can help. I get sort of excited about the idea – especially as this might solve my Mr Cartright problem too. Because coaching my sister in algebra has got to count as extra maths work, right?

In the end Carolyn says, 'Well, we can try it, I guess.' And then she says something very surprising. 'You know, I've always been so glad that I'm your older sister, and not your little one.' It's a very weird thing to say. Why would anyone want to be the younger sister? Being the youngest sucks. It must be obvious how surprised I am because Carolyn goes on to explain. 'You're way smarter than I am and it would've been hard to follow in your footsteps all the way through school. I'm lucky that you had to follow in mine instead.'

I had no idea Carolyn felt this way. It feels kind of good, to be honest. But also pretty mind-blowing. So I do what I always do when something has surprised me. I make a joke of it. 'Well, it hasn't been so easy for me either,' I say, rolling my eyes and sighing dramatically. 'Do you know how hard it is to follow in someone's footsteps when they're dancing along in high heels most of the time?'

Carolyn actually laughs – a little bit, at least – and then she looks at me, head tilted. 'I don't know about you,' she says, 'but I'm starving.'

Together we head to the kitchen. There's a jar of red pesto in the cupboard and I offer to make pasta, but Carolyn shakes her head. 'Let's make something different,' she says. 'Something totally new.'

We grab a couple of shopping bags and walk to the local shops. Carolyn buys a whole lot of things with her own money. She's like a madwoman, flinging all this stuff into our trolley. I'm not really sure what half of it is. Then we lug it all home.

'Right,' Carolyn announces as we dump the bags on the kitchen bench. 'We're making risotto.' She pulls up a recipe on her phone. In the picture is a bowl of something ricey with bits of chicken in it. It does look pretty good, except that it's got these little flecks of green stuff mixed through it. Generally I'm not big on green flecks but I'm not about to say that when Carolyn's looking semi-cheerful again.

'Have you ever made risotto before?' I ask.

'No,' says Carolyn. 'But I know it's going to be good. Trust me.'

We spend the next half-hour chopping and peeling like crazy, and then Carolyn starts cooking. And soon I can tell that she was right. The risotto smells great. I start feeling even hungrier than before. 'Maybe you could be a chef or something?' I say.

'Maybe,' says Carolyn, shrugging – but I can tell she's pleased I said it.

We're just finishing when we hear Mum's key in the door. We grin at each other. Mum takes a few steps inside, and suddenly stops. 'Oh my god!' we hear her say. 'What is that *incredible* smell?'

'We made dinner!' I call out.

Mum practically runs down the hallway. When she sees the risotto she gets a little teary and has to fan her face with a junk-mail catalogue. It's kind of weird to me that rice could make you cry, but that's my mum for you.

We make Mum sit down and I pour her a glass of juice while Carolyn serves the risotto onto three plates. She doesn't just glug it on like I would've done. She puts a neat ladle on each plate and then a little sprig of parsley to one side for decoration. It looks just like it did in the picture on her phone.

The risotto is really creamy and delicious and not at all weird to eat. Even the green flecks taste pretty good. Mum goes a bit over the top with the compliments. Apparently, it's the *most delicious* thing she's *ever* eaten.

It's not until we've eaten the entire pot of risotto, and I've cleared away the plates, and Mum's produced a block of chocolate from somewhere (which we're almost – but not quite – too full to eat), that Carolyn tells her about Max. She looks sad as she says it, but she doesn't cry this time.

Mum gives her a hug, and then pulls me into it too. 'There's something very strange going on in the world when three people as fabulous as us are single!'

It's nice the way she says it. Like the three of us are in this together. Because break-ups suck, no matter how old you are, no matter what the reasons were, no matter how long the relationship lasted. We talk about it for a while, and then Mum squeezes our hands tightly. 'We've got to look after each other. Be kind. Help each other through.' We all promise that we will.

V

I'm in my room after dinner when Mum knocks and comes in. She's holding a catalogue and she puts it on my desk in front of me. It's open to the lingerie page and one of the bras has been circled with red pen. 'What do you think of that one?' she asks. The bra doesn't have diamantés or padding, but the fabric is a pretty pearly-pink colour with darker pink swirls across it.

'I like it,' I say.

Mum looks pleased. 'Carolyn pointed it out. It's a good brand too, one that will last.'

I'm feeling kind of excited now. Because she wouldn't be showing it to me if she wasn't planning on buying it for me, right? 'I'm going to put it on layby for you,' Mum says. 'I'll pay a little bit off each month and I'll have paid the whole thing off by your birthday.'

My birthday! That's over six months away. But I know better than to complain. 'Thanks, Mum,' I say, giving her a hug. 'Could you get the 8B? I think I'll really need that size by then.'

Mum opens her mouth like she's about to disagree, then changes her mind and nods instead. 'Sure,' she says. 'Sounds like a good idea.'

Twelve

I'm kind of dreading the night of the school social. Leni and Soph must've agreed not to talk about it in front of me, but I still know it's coming up and everyone else talks about it all the time. On the Friday night I'm planning to watch a DVD, but Carolyn stays home and we end up working on her algebra stuff together. I know that spending Friday evening doing maths doesn't sound like the most fun, but it's actually fine. It's nice to spend time with Carolyn, for one thing. I'd never say it to her, of course, but I'm kind of glad that she and Max split. It means that I'm seeing a lot more of her. And we're getting along a lot better too.

It took a bit of work convincing Mr C to go along with my idea of coaching Carolyn for my 'extra maths' assignment. I think he was worried that the algebra would be too hard for me – and I have to admit, I was a bit worried too. But I can be very determined when I want to figure something out, and I really wanted to do this. I think the tipping point for Mr C was when I said I was thinking about becoming a maths teacher when I left school, and that helping my sister would be good practice. A total lie, by the way. There's no way I'd be a maths teacher.

It was difficult at first – and not just because of the algebra itself. It was mostly that to begin with, Carolyn was embarrassed about having her little sister tell her how to do stuff. But after two days, she was used to it. The good thing is that she doesn't mind asking me questions when she doesn't get something. She says that sometimes in class, Mr Cartright goes really fast and she's always too embarrassed to put up her hand and admit she didn't understand it. And then she's even *further* behind.

So like I said, on the night of the school social, Carolyn spends most of the evening in my room, working. She's doing pretty well but I can tell she's getting tired. Eventually she shuts her book and says, 'That's enough for now.'

I check the time. It's 9.30. The social will be finishing soon. It makes me feel a little sad. 'Wanna watch a DVD or something?' I suggest. I need distractions. I'm still not allowed to have my friends over for a DVD night, but surely it doesn't matter if I watch one with my sister.

'No,' says Carolyn, smiling in this mysterious way. 'Now it's time for me to teach *you* something.' Then she disappears off to her room, returning a few minutes later with her bulging make-up kit. She pulls out my desk chair. 'I'm going to show you how to put on make-up so that none of the teachers notice you're wearing it,' she tells me. 'Then you won't have to wipe it all off before recess.'

I don't really think this is possible, but Carolyn sets to work with her little brushes and tubes and I just let her go for it. She flicks on my radio and sings along, although whenever I try to join in too, she tells me to sit still. Eventually she lets me look at myself in the mirror, and I'm pretty impressed. She's put on the make-up in this subtle way that makes me look good, without being too obvious.

I'm just getting her to show me how she did it when there's a knock at my bedroom door. 'Come in, Mum!' I call, figuring it has to be her. But it's not – it's Leni and Soph, all dressed up in their clothes for the social. Soph has on a purple tie-dyed maxi dress and Leni – who only *ever* wears jeans – is wearing a short flippy skirt (which I gave her because I knew it'd suit her) and leggings. I feel a little pang looking at them, thinking that I missed out on all the fun of dressing up and going to the social with them.

'Hi!' says Leni, hugging me before she throws herself on my bed. 'Mind if I take my shoes off? They're killing me.'

'Sure,' I say. 'But what are you guys doing here?'

Soph and Leni grin at me. 'We left a bit early,' says Soph.

'Because we were dying to see you!' finished Leni. 'It just didn't feel right without you there at the social.' I'm happy they're here – *really* happy – but something's bothering me.

'I'm not allowed to have anyone over,' I remind them. 'My parents are punishing me until the next millennium, remember?'

'Your mum let us in, you doof!' Soph says.

'She said we could stay for a bit,' explains Leni. 'We have something to show you, you see.' She pulls a Flip video camera from her bag.

'I've seen your mum's camera before, Leni,' I say, even though I know she's talking about what's *on* the camera. Leni puts it on and we all crowd around – even Carolyn.

My friends – my sweet, funny, awesome friends – have made a film of the social so I can see what it was like. They have taken it in turns to record different things and do the commentary. They've filmed the fairy lights strung across the front gate. They've filmed the outside of the hall with the 'welcome' banner above the door. And they've also recorded a message for me from pretty much everyone in our entire year level. It's kind of embarrassing, but it's also nice.

A lot of people say the same thing. Most of the girls say, 'Hi, Anya! Sorry you can't make it – it's SO awesome!' Most of the boys say, 'You're lucky you got out of it.' But I can tell they're mostly enjoying themselves, even if they're pretending that they're not.

A few people say different things, though. Like Edi, for instance. She says, 'It's not the same without you here,

Anya.' Which makes me feel good.

Then suddenly Leni stops the camera. 'The next bit is Ethan,' she says. 'Do you want to see it?'

'You actually got him to talk on the video?' I say, my stomach rolling like a wave.

'Soph *made* him,' says Leni. 'After she gave him a huge serve about dropping people via text messages.'

I turn to Soph. 'You did that?' I ask, starting to laugh.

'Of course I did,' says Soph. 'I've been meaning to for ages – I just had to find the right time.' She shakes her fist. 'No-one dumps my friend like that and gets away with it.'

Leni shakes her head, laughing. 'You should've seen him, Anya,' she says. 'He was shaking in his shoes by the time Soph finished with him.'

'So,' says Soph. 'Do you want to see what he said?'

My stomach rolls again. 'Yes,' I say. 'No. I'm not sure.'

'Go on,' says Carolyn. 'You should.'

So Leni presses play and suddenly there's Ethan, his nervous-looking face filling the screen. I notice that he's dropped most of the *improvements* I made to him. His hair is back to how it was and he's wearing a terrible shirt, but the funny thing is, it kind of suits him.

'Go *on*, Ethan,' I hear Soph's voice saying sternly off-camera. 'Talk.'

Ethan coughs. 'Hi, Anya,' he says. 'Sorry you couldn't come tonight because I know you were really looking forward to it. But don't worry, you're not missing much. The food is terrible and so is the music.' It's funny, though, because as he's speaking I hear one of my favourite songs playing in the background. And as he talks, I realise that I'm not feeling so bad about the break-up anymore. I guess I'm over it. Pretty much.

Ethan stops talking and I hear Soph say, 'Isn't there anything else you want to say?'

And then Ethan's expression changes. 'Actually,' he says. 'Yes, there is.'

'Well, go on, say it,' says Soph.

I guess I'm expecting him to apologise for text-dumping me, but instead he says, 'Anya, I know you got the highest mark in our class for the last test. And Mr C told me you're helping Carolyn with algebra. So I'm wondering if we could be study buddies.'

I shake my head. 'Do you believe the nerve of this guy?' I say. 'First he dumps me because I'm *not smart enough* and now he wants me to *help him study!*'

A song comes on the radio and Carolyn suddenly jumps up to dance, swaying in time to the music. I know it's one of her current favourites and I like it too. It's meaningful, you know? And true. It's a song about how when someone breaks your heart, your friends will be the ones to help you put the pieces back together. Someone like Ethan would probably say it was a cliché, and maybe he's right, but I actually don't care. Right now it feels true to me.

Leni gets up next and starts dancing in that long-legged, spider-like way of hers, and even Soph joins in, swirling around, jumping on and off my bed in a kind of crazy gypsy dance. It's funny because in one way we're all off in our own little worlds, doing our own dances, but in another way it feels like we're dancing together too. I know that sounds confusing, and maybe impossible, but that's how it is. And it just feels right somehow. Like life, I guess.